# The ___
## of the Ruby Gazelle

Nancy took one slow step at a time, trying not to make too much noise. Somewhere ahead, she again heard the rustling of feet in the leaves.

"Hello? Are you the—"

She heard another pair of footsteps crashing through the brush from the direction of the carousel. They were coming from behind, heading straight for her!

"Who . . . ?" Nancy whirled, blinking into the darkness. "Bess? George? Zoe? Is that . . ."

She caught a fleeting glimpse of a hulking shadow charging toward her. A split second later, she felt a painful blow to the side of her head. The last thing she remembered was the jellylike feeling in her legs as she slipped senselessly to the ground. . . .

# Nancy Drew
# Mystery Stories

## Available from MINSTREL Books

# NANCY DREW® 135

## THE RIDDLE OF THE RUBY GAZELLE

### CAROLYN KEENE

A MINSTREL® BOOK

Published by POCKET BOOKS
New York   London   Toronto   Sydney   Tokyo   Singapore

This book is a work of fiction. Names, characters, places and
incidents are products of the author's imagination or are used
fictitiously. Any resemblance to actual events or locales or persons
living or dead is entirely coincidental.

A MINSTREL PAPERBACK *Original*

A Minstrel Book published by
POCKET BOOKS, a division of Simon & Schuster Inc.
1230 Avenue of the Americas, New York, NY 10020

Copyright © 1997 by Simon & Schuster Inc.
Produced by Mega-Books, Inc.

ISBN: 0-671-00048-9

First Minstrel Books printing February 1997

10  9  8  7  6  5  4  3

NANCY DREW, NANCY DREW MYSTERY STORIES,
A MINSTREL BOOK and colophon are registered
trademarks of Simon & Schuster Inc.

Cover art by Doron Ben-Ami

Printed in the U.S.A.

# Contents

# 1

## Trouble Under the Brooklyn Bridge

"I had no idea the view from the Brooklyn Bridge was so amazing!" George Fayne said. Her brown eyes sparkled as she turned to grin at her best friends, Nancy Drew and Bess Marvin. She flung out one arm and pointed across the East River. "The Empire State Building, the World Trade Center, South Street Seaport. You can see it all from here."

"The view *is* gorgeous," Nancy said. She flipped up the collar of her parka and leaned against the railing of the pedestrian boardwalk on the bridge. Far below, past the rushing cars, sunlight danced on the water while a tugboat pulled a barge down the river. The Staten Island Ferry was moving with the Statue of Liberty in the distance. A cold wind whipped up from the water, sending Nancy's reddish blond hair flying around her face.

1

"Photo op!" Bess called out. "Over there, you guys, with the World Trade Center behind you." She snapped a shot, then turned to the tall young woman who was with them. "You don't know how lucky you are, Zoe. You get to look at the Manhattan skyline every day."

"You get used to it when you live here," Zoe said, letting out a laugh. Her wavy black hair spilled over the collar of her red wool coat, and her laugh was so infectious that Nancy couldn't help grinning back.

Zoe Krieger lived in Brooklyn Heights, right across the river from Manhattan. Nancy, Bess, and George had gotten to know her the summer before, when Zoe was visiting relatives in River Heights. When Zoe invited them to stay with her in Brooklyn, all three young women had jumped at the chance. They'd arrived just that morning, and Zoe had decided to start their visit with a walk partway across the famous bridge.

"Anyway, we're here to see Brooklyn, not Manhattan," George pointed out.

Nancy, Bess, and George usually stayed with Nancy's aunt Eloise in Manhattan when they visited New York City. "It's too bad that Aunt Eloise is on a cruise, and we won't get to see her," Nancy said. "But I'm glad to get to know a different part of the city *and* help out with the benefit you were telling us about, Zoe. Didn't you say you're trying to raise money to renovate a park in your neighborhood?"

Zoe nodded. "The Heights Gardens," she said. "It's a small but beautiful old park. With city

2

funding being cut back all the time, it's gotten run-down. A lot of people want to destroy it and put up new buildings."

"*More* buildings? It seems as if there's already enough concrete around." Bess shot a surprised glance at the Brooklyn side of the bridge. Docks, industrial buildings, and a highway lined the river. The ground rose up sharply behind them, and on top of a bluff sat row after row of townhouses, apartment houses, and a long promenade overlooking the river. Cars roared on a highway under the Promenade. "You'd think people would do all they could to save a park."

"Unfortunately, not everyone in Brooklyn Heights feels the way you do," Zoe said, frowning. "A theater group wanted to build a new theater there. Local businesses wanted a parking garage. The neighborhood hospital planned to use the space for a new wing. You can see the Heights Gardens from here, actually," she went on. "Where all those trees are."

Nancy looked in the direction where Zoe was pointing and saw, amid the buildings on the bluff, a patch of green that took up half a city block. Brick and brownstone houses ringed the park on three sides.

"How could anyone think of destroying it?" Bess asked.

Nancy had to agree. "A hospital wing and a new theater sound like good causes, but—couldn't people find room for those things without wrecking the park?"

"They'll have to now," Zoe said with a determined nod as she led the girls back toward Brooklyn on the walkway. "Luckily, we have a strong neighborhood association, the Brooklyn Heights Coalition. They signed petitions, held rallies, called our local politicians. Students from my high school got involved, too. We went door-to-door to talk to people about it, and in the end we won. The city council voted to save the park."

"That's great!" Bess said.

"Definitely." Zoe grinned, then raised an eyebrow at Nancy, Bess, and George. "The only problem is, the city didn't give us enough money for the renovation."

"Which is why you're throwing the benefit, right?" George asked. Her cheeks were ruddy from the cold, and the ends of her curly brown hair blew out from beneath her beret.

"Yup. There's going to be a concert on Friday and an auction Saturday. Since my school's on vacation this week, we'll have lots of time to help get everything ready," Zoe answered. "There's going to be tons of local memorabilia at the auction. But what I'm really looking forward to is the concert. The Raving Lunatics are playing, and it's going to be great!"

"The Raving Lunatics?" Bess echoed. "I think I've heard of them. Aren't they the ones who just came out with that song 'Gravity to Go-Go'?"

Zoe nodded proudly. "That's them. They're from

4

Brooklyn Heights. They've been playing in cafes and clubs around here for years, but they just signed a recording contract. 'Gravity to Go-Go' is their first song to make it to the national charts. Randy told me that their recording company might even arrange for them to do a tour with a major band."

"Randy?" Nancy asked.

"Oh—sorry. I forgot that you don't know him yet," Zoe said. "Randy La Guardia. He's the Lunatics' lead singer. He and the rest of the band are seniors with me at Bradley Prep."

Nancy knew that Bradley Prep was the private high school Zoe attended. "Sounds great. I can't wait until Friday's concert to hear them," she said.

"We don't have to wait that long," Zoe told her, her brown eyes sparkling. "The Lunatics are practicing in the Anchorage right now, as a matter of fact. Do you want to go?"

"Definitely!" Bess crowed.

"Sure," Nancy said. "But what's the Anchorage?"

Zoe pointed toward the end of the Brooklyn Bridge. "The Brooklyn Anchorage—where the support cables of the bridge are anchored," she said. "A network of cables, metal girders, and stone support walls are built inside the base of the bridge. It sounds weird, but it's amazing. Inside it's big enough for performances, skateboard competitions, stuff like that. The city schedules different events."

"Sounds great," George said.

"It is," Zoe said. "Usually, the Anchorage isn't open during the winter, but Mrs. O'Neill got permission to hold the benefit concert and auction there. She's the president of the Brooklyn Heights Coalition, and she's in charge of organizing the benefit." Zoe shook her head in amazement, brushing back her hair. "Actually, Mrs. O. is one of the reasons so many kids from Bradley Prep got involved trying to save the Heights Gardens. She's interested in teenagers—volunteering in youth groups, organizing programs for students to work for charities and all kinds of local businesses. But you can see for yourself how great she is. She's probably at the Anchorage."

When they came to the end of the bridge, Zoe led Nancy, Bess, and George off the pedestrian walkway. A side street sloped down a hill back toward the river, and the girls followed it for several blocks. Thick walls of stone stretched to the ground beneath the bridge while traffic roared overhead. Nancy spotted metal double doors set into the wall of the base of the bridge. A metal sculpture stood in front, along with the frozen remains of a small garden. The doors were open, and rock music blared from inside.

"They're playing 'Gravity to Go-Go'!" Bess said.

"Then we'd better *go-go* inside," George said.

As soon as they stepped through the metal doors, out of the wind, Nancy felt warmer. All around were windowless golden brick walls that rose up, curving into vaulted ceilings. Electric lights were anchored into the brick.

"Wow. This place *is* amazing," she said.

"You haven't seen anything yet," Zoe said.

"There's a maze of rooms and tunnels that never get used. I've heard that you could spend hours exploring and still not see it all."

Zoe headed left through an arch to a cavernous open space. At the far end of it, a stage was set up against another brick wall. Nancy spotted a ramp that led deeper into the Anchorage. Three young men and a young woman were on the stage amid a jumble of amplifiers, microphones, guitars, drums, and an electric piano. They were playing and singing so intently that they didn't seem to notice the teenagers who had gathered to hear them. Dozens of folding metal chairs were stacked against the walls. Space heaters had been set up, as well. They gave off just enough warmth to take the chill from the air.

"Fantastic," George said under her breath.

"I don't know whether you're talking about the music or the Anchorage," Nancy said, grinning. "As far as I'm concerned, they're both awesome!" As they joined the other spectators, she couldn't help nodding her head to the beat. When the song ended, she clapped and hooted along with everyone else.

"Looks like they're taking a break," Zoe said. "Come on. I want you guys to meet Randy and the rest of the band."

Once they were up on the stage, she led them over to the lead singer. He had dark brown hair and wore jeans and a plum-colored corduroy shirt. He was just unplugging his electric guitar. When he looked up at them, Nancy saw that he had bright blue eyes that contrasted with his dark brows and olive skin.

"Hey, Zoe," he said easily. Then he smiled at Nancy, Bess, and George. "Let me guess. You three must be the friends Zoe was telling me about. Nancy, George, and . . ." He closed his eyes and snapped his fingers a few times.

"Bess," Bess said, grinning. "You must be Randy La Guardia. You guys sound terrific!"

"Thanks. I just hope we raise enough money to fix up the Heights Gardens," Randy said.

Zoe punched him playfully on the arm and said, "You will. We've already sold most of the tickets. This place is going to be packed on Friday night—"

She broke off as she was pushed to the side by a young woman who elbowed her way toward Randy. She was petite, with blue eyes, chin-length blond hair, bangs, and an angry look on her face.

"Um, hi, Allison," Randy said, looking uncomfortable. "How's it going?"

Allison jabbed a finger toward him. "You've got a lot of nerve, Randy."

Nancy exchanged uneasy glances with Bess and George. What was going on?

"Look, Allison," Randy began, holding up his hands defensively. "I don't know what—"

"You sleazoid," Allison cried. Her fists were clenched, and her face grew redder every second. "I'm going to make you sorry for what you did to me. Sorrier than you've ever been in your life!"

# 2

## *Friends—and Enemies*

Nancy's body tensed as Allison took another step toward Randy. For an awful moment, she was afraid Allison might hit Randy.

Zoe spoke up. "Back off, Allison." Her voice was calm, but Nancy saw the tense set of her face. She stepped smoothly in front of Randy and held up a hand to Allison. "We're all trying to work *together* to raise money for the Heights Gardens, remember?"

Nancy wasn't sure how long Allison stood there, glaring. Finally, she blinked and let out her breath in an angry rush. "Fine," Allison snapped. Then she turned on her heel, stomped down the stairs from the stage, and strode angrily toward the arch leading out of the Anchorage.

"Phew!" Bess said, as soon as Allison was gone. "What was that all about?"

"Let's just say that Allison's not exactly my biggest fan," Randy said slowly, staring after Allison. "She's hated me ever since—"

"Are you all right, Randy?" one of the other band members spoke up. He was tall and lanky, with straight sandy hair that fell over his forehead. He and the two other musicians hurried over to Randy.

"I guess Allison still hasn't forgiven you for replacing her in the band," said the young woman, shaking her head. She had beautiful long, straight red hair.

"I guess not," Randy said. Turning to Nancy, Bess, and George, he said, "Meet Peter Hanson, Julio Greco, and Nina Sherman. Peter plays bass," he said, nodding toward the young blond man. "Nina's on electric piano . . ."

"And I'm on drums," Julio finished with a smile. He was shorter than Randy and Peter, with sparkling brown eyes. "Nice to meet you."

"Same here," Nancy said.

Zoe introduced Nancy, Bess, and George, then said, "Allison Demar goes to Bradley with us. She used to be the Lunatics' lead singer, but about a year ago the band voted to replace her with Randy."

"It wasn't anything personal," Peter added, pushing his hair off his forehead. "Randy's a much better singer and guitar player, that's all."

"But Allison doesn't agree?" George asked.

10

"You got it," Nina said. "She's convinced that she's the hottest musical talent on the planet."

"And she blames me personally for trying to wreck her career as a rock-and-roll star," Randy said. He shrugged, shoving his hands in his pockets. "This isn't the first time she's said stuff like that to me, but I don't take it seriously."

He glanced to the other side of the open space, where a bearded man was wheeling a dolly loaded with cardboard through the arch. "Looks like there's another delivery for the auction," he said.

"Which means that Mrs. O'Neill could probably use some help," Zoe put in. "Maybe we can all go out for pizza later?"

Randy turned to the other band members, who nodded. "Sounds good," Randy said. "We'll meet up after we're done practicing."

Nancy, Bess, and George followed Zoe through the opening in the stone wall behind the stage. A long hallway disappeared into darkness ahead. To their right, a doorway was cut into one of the massive stone walls. As Nancy stepped through it behind Zoe, she found herself in a room filled with old furniture, clothes, and boxes of toys, books, photographs, and other memorabilia. The bearded man they'd seen with the dolly was in the center of the room. With him were a gray-haired woman and a blond boy who looked about Zoe's age. The three of them were unloading the boxes from the dolly.

Nancy glanced at an old-fashioned barbershop chair to her left. The chrome was sculpted into

11

sleek swirls around the cracked red leather uphol-
stery of the seat, footrest, and headrest. "That's a
real beauty," she commented. "I'd like to buy it
myself."

"Except that I doubt you'd be allowed to bring it
home with us on the plane," Bess said with a
giggle. She nodded toward a cardboard box over-
flowing with antique dolls in old-fashioned, ruffled
clothes. "I'd take one of those, though. Some of
them look as if they could be over a hundred years
old."

George stepped over to a baseball shirt hanging
from a portable rack. "Check out the Brooklyn
Dodgers jersey," she said. "This is a real collector's
item. I bet it'll bring in a high price."

"That's what we're counting on," a voice said
from behind them.

Nancy looked up to see the gray-haired woman
standing right behind her. Both taller and heavier
than Nancy, she was wearing jeans, a baggy red
sweater, and worn and dirty work gloves. She had a
warm, round face and lively hazel eyes that made
her seem youthful.

"We're going to need every penny we can get to
restore the Heights Gardens," the woman went on.
"Not to mention all the help we can get." She eyed
Nancy, Bess, and George curiously. "You three
aren't here to volunteer, by any chance, are you?"
she asked.

"Absolutely," Nancy said, grinning.

"Meet Mrs. O'Neill, you guys. She's always looking for new victims to help her get everything ready for the benefit," Zoe said. "Mrs. O., these are my friends Nancy, Bess, and George. We have the rest of the afternoon to help out."

Mrs. O'Neill gave them a pleased smile. "Great. You can start by cataloging the things Sam Altman is donating from his secondhand store." Going over to a canvas tote bag on the floor next to the arch, she pulled out a pad of paper, a pile of paper tags, and some pens. "Each item needs to be tagged with a number and written down here on my list. There'll be more, too. Sam and Vic just went to get another load from Sam's truck."

"Vic Wollenski is another senior at Bradley," Zoe said. "He's been helping out with the Heights Gardens benefit, too."

A few moments later, Vic and the bearded man returned with two more dollies, each loaded with an enormous cast-iron animal. Mr. Altman's dolly held a six-foot-high green giraffe with yellow spots. The animal on Vic's dolly was a gazelle, glazed a deep ruby red with purple horns and stripes. Both animals were pitted with rust spots and were somewhat charred, as if they'd been burned. But Nancy was struck by how fanciful and unusual they were.

"Those are beautiful!" Bess exclaimed.

"And heavy," Vic said. He had curly blond hair and the compact, muscular build of a wrestler. After unhooking the strap that tied the gazelle to the dolly, he eased the dolly out from under the animal. "There's still one to go."

He left, and when he came back, he was wheeling a dark blue tiger with orange stripes. It, too, had some burned and rusted areas.

"These are quite something!" Mrs. O'Neill said. A faraway look came into her eyes as she scrutinized the animals, taking in every detail. "I can't believe it's possible. You certainly don't see anything like these nowadays."

"Where did they come from?" George asked.

"These creatures were once part of the Jungle Carousel at Coney Island," Mr. Altman said. "The carousel was ruined in a fire back in 1941." He pressed a finger to a small hole next to the gazelle's ears. "I'm afraid the leather reins and tail were burned, and the animals have corroded some with age. These are the only survivors of the fire I know of. They've been in my store since before I took it over from my father . . . over thirty years ago."

Waving a hand at the other boxes, he added, "The rest are photos of Brooklyn, furniture, a few old roller skates. My niece goes to Bradley Prep. When she told me about the auction, I thought maybe this would help bring in a few extra pennies."

"It'll bring in more than that," Mrs. O'Neill said. "Thank you so much, Mr. Altman."

"Glad to help," he told her. He glanced at the cardboard boxes and let out a chuckle. "You know, this stuff was considered junk years ago," he said. "People like my father and grandfather collected it just because they liked the looks of it."

14

"Now they're called antiques," Zoe said. "People are willing to pay a lot of money to own a piece of Brooklyn's past. At least, that's what we're hoping."

"Well, I'd better be off," Mr. Altman said. He stacked the two empty dollies and wheeled them out the door. "Good luck!"

His last words were drowned out as the Raving Lunatics began rehearsing again. Nancy began nodding her head to the music, but she noticed a slight frown on Mrs. O'Neill's face.

"I know you kids all love rock music, but I just can't get used to the relentless, pounding noise," Mrs. O'Neill said. She gave a self-conscious laugh, then bent over one of the boxes Mr. Altman had just delivered. "I guess I'm showing my age, but to be perfectly honest, I'd prefer a concert by my husband's barbershop quartet to this racket."

"I'm with you, Mrs. O.," Vic Wollenski spoke up as he untaped and opened a second box. "I wouldn't even go to the concert if we weren't raising money for a good cause."

Nancy looked at him in surprise. "You don't like the Raving Lunatics?" she asked.

Vic raked a hand through his curly blond hair, his eyes playing moodily over the room. "They're okay, I guess," he said. "Except Randy. What a jerk. That guy has a totally inflated opinion of himself."

"Randy happens to be one of my best friends," Zoe said, turning an annoyed look on Vic. "You don't know what you're talking about!"

15

"I know *exactly* what I'm talking about," he shot back. "For your information—"

"Calm down, you two," Mrs. O'Neill cut in. She looked firmly from Zoe to Vic. "We have work to do."

Vic backed off, but Nancy noticed that the look on his face remained ice-cold. She, Zoe, George, and Bess started to remove old photographs from one of the boxes Mr. Altman had brought. George leaned forward and whispered to Zoe, "Randy didn't seem stuck-up to me."

"Or to me," Nancy said. "Randy was really friendly to us." Most of the kids seemed to like him *and* the Raving Lunatics, she thought. But Vic and Allison were proof that Randy also had a few enemies.

"Am I dreaming, or is this the best pizza in the world?" Bess asked that evening.

Nancy bit into a crusty slice topped with sausage, roasted red peppers, creamy mozzarella cheese, and fresh basil. "You're definitely not dreaming," she told Bess. "It's delicious!"

"Pete's is the best pizza place around," Randy said, grinning across the table at the girls. "Their secret is the coal-stoked brick oven."

Nancy, Bess, George, and Zoe had spent the afternoon helping Mrs. O'Neill to label and catalog items for Saturday's auction. They were just finishing up when the Raving Lunatics stopped practicing. Randy and Zoe had both insisted that they eat at Pete's, one of the oldest pizzerias in Brooklyn. It was located in a brick building just off the Heights Gardens. Nancy had to admit that the place had a lot of charm, with its red-checked tablecloths and wood wainscoting. The walls were lined with signed photographs of all the famous people who had eaten there. Every table was filled.

"Maybe we should serve Pete's pizza when we play on Friday night," Julio suggested. He plucked a bit of sausage from his plate and popped it into his mouth. "Then we'll be sure to get a full house."

"It's not a bad idea, but you guys don't need gimmicks to get a sellout crowd," Zoe said. "The concert isn't for another four days, and we've already sold a lot of the tickets."

Nina brushed her hair behind her ears. "If we do well at the auction, too, we should have enough money to completely renovate the Heights Gardens."

Nancy glanced out the window at the park. A marble gazebo with chipped columns was at the center of the park. Brick paths with broken-down benches wound through the scraggly, overgrown shrubs and trees. Nancy made out a bronze statue at one end of the park and a fountain at the other—both covered with graffiti. Although the park needed repairs, she was struck by how elegant and graceful it was. It fit perfectly with the charming, historic townhouses of the surrounding tree-lined streets. "You guys must be proud of all the work you're doing."

17

An orange light lit up one end of the Heights Gardens. It took Nancy a second to realize where the light was coming from. When she did, her whole body filled with dread.

"Those are flames, you guys," she said in shock.

"What!" everyone else cried at once, whipping their heads around to look.

Red-orange flames leaped a dozen feet into the sky, licking at the bare branches of the trees. "Oh, no," Zoe cried. "The Heights Gardens are on fire!"

# 3

## *Fire!*

Nancy jumped to her feet, threw some money on the table, and ran for the door. "We've got to do something. Come on!"

"I'm right behind you, Nancy!" George cried.

"I'll call the fire department," Nina said.

Nancy heard a lot of commotion in the restaurant as the others followed, but she didn't stop to look behind her. She wasn't sure what they could do, but somehow they had to make sure the fire didn't destroy the beautiful old park.

It wasn't until she bolted through the door and across the street that she noticed the crowd of people gathered in the park. "What's going on?" Zoe asked. She ran up beside Nancy, her face tight with worry, and began elbowing her way through the thick crowd. "Let us through!" she demanded.

All of Nancy's attention was focused on the fire. It hadn't actually reached the trees yet, she saw with relief. But the crowd of people made it impossible to see exactly what was burning. If they could only get a little closer . . .

Nancy veered around a knot of people, then let out the breath she'd been holding. She could finally see the bottom of the fire, and it *wasn't* burning out of control. It was contained in a large metal bin.

"Thank goodness!" Zoe said, coming to a halt next to Nancy. Seconds later George, Bess, Randy, Peter, and Julio crowded up behind them.

"I don't get it," Bess said, trying to catch her breath. "Where did all these people come from? Why is everyone wearing those skeleton costumes?"

"Costumes?" Nancy echoed. She looked around in surprise. She'd been so busy watching the fire that she hadn't paid much attention to the people. Now she saw that about twenty men and women were dressed as skeletons. They wore dark clothes with skeleton bones painted on in a luminous green. Their papier-mâché masks were painted with ghoulish skeleton faces that reflected the glow from the fire.

"I'm not sure what it's all about, but at least they're not trying to burn down the park," Nancy said as she took it all in.

A figure at the front of the group pounded a drum in a slow, haunting beat while the others carried a cardboard coffin toward the fire. Some words were painted on the coffin in white. Nancy had to squint to make them out.

"The Brooklyn Players," George read, beating her to it. She turned to Zoe and asked, "Is this some kind of a joke?"

"Shhh!" Bess hissed. "I think he heard you."

The man with the drum shot George an annoyed glance. "Laugh if you will, but this is a sad day for the Brooklyn Players," he said in a deep, dramatic voice. "Tonight our theater closes its doors for all time."

"Why?" one of the spectators called out.

"Our landlord is converting the theater to a multiplex cinema," the man answered. "Unless the Brooklyn Players can find a new home, we are as good as dead."

At that, the players all erupted into ghoulish wails. As they guided the cardboard coffin into the metal container, the flames leaped higher into the sky. Nancy knew it was just a theatrical demonstration, but she had to admit it was effective. The man with the drum took off his mask to watch more closely.

"That's Tim Chang," Zoe whispered, frowning. "He's the director of the Brooklyn Players. They're the theater group I mentioned, the one that wanted to build a theater instead of renovating the park."

Tim had an athletic build and he wasn't much taller than Nancy, but his costume and deep, booming voice made him seem larger than life.

"We've already lost our fight to have a new

theater built here to replace this run-down weed patch that calls itself a park," Tim went on.

"Weed patch!" Randy said under his breath. "The Heights Gardens is a lot more important to the neighborhood than any half-baked theater group."

Most of the people around them didn't appear to have heard Randy. They were busy watching the Brooklyn Players wail and dance around the fire. But apparently Tim *had* heard. He looked right at Randy. While the actors continued their performance, he stepped over and gave Randy a cool once-over.

"You're one of the Raving Lunatics, aren't you?" Tim asked. "I've seen your photo on the posters for that ridiculous benefit being held this weekend."

"We're all helping out with the benefit to renovate the park," Randy answered, crossing his arms over his chest.

Tim took them all in with his intense gaze. "The Raving Lunatics seems like the perfect name for you," he said sarcastically. "You must be mad, trying to save a few trees instead of supporting an important cultural group like mine."

Randy opened his mouth to say something, but Zoe stopped him. "Forget it, Randy," she told him. "Let's just get out of here."

"Fine," Randy snapped.

As Randy started to turn away, Tim gave an exaggerated bow. "It was a pleasure meeting you," he said in a voice that was anything but sincere. "I hope you won't mind if I don't wish you good luck. The truth is, I hope the entire benefit flops."

"There's no way that's going to happen," George said. "Not with the Lunatics playing."

Tim turned back to the fire.

"That guy's crazy," Randy said, shaking his head. "But he *is* right about one thing. We'll have to work hard to make sure we put on a show people will like." He reached into his pocket and pulled out a key. "I was thinking of going back to the Anchorage tonight to work on a new song I've been writing. Maybe I'll get it in good enough shape to play at the concert."

"You're going now?" Zoe asked. "But the Anchorage will be deserted."

"That's what I'm counting on," Randy said, a smile curving his lips. "The quiet will help me concentrate better."

"Whatever," Peter said. "Just don't stay out too late. Remember, we're all going on a cruise of New York harbor first thing tomorrow."

"A cruise?" Bess asked, her eyes lighting up.

Zoe turned to Bess with a smile. "I guess I forgot to mention that," she said. "Mrs. O'Neill arranged it. She figured it would be a fun way to kick off the benefit—and treat ourselves for all the hard work we've done."

"Don't worry, I'll be there," Randy said, stepping away from the demonstrators.

Nancy started to follow him, but a prickly feeling at the back of her head made her turn around. Tim was a few feet away from them, she saw. He had taken off his mask, and he was looking at Randy with daggers in his eyes.

"Wake up, sleepyhead."

Nancy heard George's voice calling, but it sounded as if it were coming from far away. "Mmmphff," she mumbled, rolling over and pulling her pillow over her head.

The next thing she knew, the pillow was being plucked away from her, and she felt warm sunlight on her face. When she finally opened her eyes, George was standing next to her in the guest room they were sharing with Bess. George was already dressed in jeans and a sweater. She grinned and tossed the pillow lightly back to Nancy.

"Come on. Zoe and Bess are eating breakfast. It's nine, and we have to be down at the waterfront by ten for the harbor cruise," George said.

"That's right." Nancy pushed herself up and sat, yawning and rubbing her eyes. "I can't believe I slept so late. I'll be out in a minute."

She'd been up until after two in the morning. Every time she'd started to drift off, she'd remembered the steely look in Tim's eyes or the way Allison had threatened Randy. And then she'd be wide awake again. She kept telling herself there was probably nothing to worry about. But she hadn't been able to shake her nervousness.

I'm not going to let it keep me from enjoying the harbor tour, she told herself firmly.

A quick shower and a bagel, cream cheese, and orange juice helped Nancy to feel refreshed. Forty-five minutes later, she, Zoe, Bess, and George were walking down the steps of Zoe's brownstone house.

"The Harbor Tours pier isn't far from the Anchorage," Zoe said. She headed down the tree-lined street. "This way."

Zoe led them down the street, past a church and dozens of quaint brick and brownstone houses with elaborate wrought iron railings and gates. They were heading toward the East River, Nancy realized. She caught sight of a patch of water beyond a railing ahead of them.

"How beautiful!" Bess exclaimed as they reached the end of the street.

A wide walkway overlooked the river in front of them. It was several blocks long and filled with joggers, dog walkers, and men and women reading newspapers on benches in the morning sunlight. Beyond the railing were the spectacular sights of Lower Manhattan, just across the river, as well as of the Statue of Liberty, Ellis Island, and the Brooklyn Bridge. The view as far as the New Jersey mountains was so striking that Nancy stopped short to take it all in. "Wow" was all she could say.

"This is the Promenade," Zoe said, gesturing to the walkway. "From here you get the best view there is of New York City—not that the tour of the harbor won't be great," she added. "The boat goes around New York harbor. The view of the tip of Manhattan is fantastic, and we'll get right up close to Ellis Island and the Statue of Liberty."

"What a great way to get everyone psyched for the benefit," Bess said.

Zoe nodded. "There's more work to do, but" — she flipped up the collar of her coat, grinning at Nancy, Bess, and George — "it's time for us to start having fun!"

"Absolutely," Nancy said, laughing.

Zoe turned right onto a steeply sloping road that led downhill from the park and the Promenade. When they reached the bottom of the hill, Zoe turned left onto the street that ran alongside the Anchorage. The road sloped down toward the water. As soon as Nancy rounded the corner, she saw a tour boat moored at a pier next to the East River. A group of people had already gathered there, including Mrs. O'Neill. With her canvas bag slung over the shoulder of her down coat, she was standing next to the ticket office, along with two other middle-aged women.

Nancy spotted Nina's red hair among the crowd. She was standing with Julio, and they both kept glancing toward the street. "Have you seen Randy and Peter?" Nina asked, when Zoe, Nancy, Bess, and George came up to them. "They were supposed to meet us here half an hour ago so we could take some publicity photos of the band before the tour."

Zoe shook her head. "It's ten o'clock now," she said, checking her watch. "That's weird. It's not like the guys to be late."

"Well, they'd better hurry up," George said, "or they're going to miss the tour altogether."

Just then, Nancy spotted Peter Hanson's tall, lanky figure running down the street toward the pier. His jacket was unzipped, and his face was flushed and sweaty. "Here comes Peter, anyway," she said.

"You're just in time!" Julio called out. "Where's Randy?"

Peter was so out of breath from running that he couldn't even talk at first. He bent with his hands braced on his knees, taking in huge gulps of air. "I don't know . . . where Randy is," he finally answered. "He was supposed to pick me up this morning, but he never showed. I just called his folks, but they said he never came home last night, and he hasn't called." He brushed back the shock of blond hair that had fallen over his forehead and shot a sober glance around the group. "They're pretty worried."

So was Nancy. All her concerns from the night before bubbled up again. Don't jump to conclusions, she reminded herself. There could be a reasonable explanation for why Randy isn't here yet.

"Maybe he just stayed up all night with some friends?" she suggested.

Zoe shook her head firmly. "That's not like Randy. He's super-responsible. He would at least call his parents."

"And he'd never skip out on his band duties, like taking photos this morning," Nina added.

"Sounds serious," Bess said, biting her lip. "Should we call the police?"

"Maybe we should check the Anchorage first," Nancy suggested. "That's where Randy said he was going last night. Maybe he fell asleep there and hasn't woken up yet."

Peter nodded. "Could be." He looked around at Mrs. O'Neill and the other students. "We don't want to alarm everyone for no reason, though," he said. "Maybe Nina, Julio, and I should stay here. We'll tell Mrs. O. what's going on."

While the band members went over to Mrs. O'Neill, Nancy, Bess, George, and Zoe hurried from the pier and up the street to the Anchorage. The double doors were closed, but when George yanked on one, it pulled open easily.

"It's not locked," Zoe said, looking hopeful. "Maybe Randy *is* here."

The lights were on, too, Nancy saw. But she didn't hear anyone inside.

"Randy?" Zoe called out. When no one answered, she ran ahead. "Randy! Are you here?"

Nancy, Bess, and George raced after her to the area where the band had been practicing the day before. Zoe was already up on the stage, holding a guitar plugged into an amplifier. Next to her was the open guitar case.

"I don't get it," she said, looking down from the stage. "Randy's nowhere around, but here's his guitar." Raising her voice, she called Randy's name again. "Randy! Are you here? Answer me, *please!*"

The only answer was the sound of her own voice echoing through the Anchorage.

"Maybe he left his guitar there after he finished working on the song last night?" Bess said.

Nancy jogged up the stairs to the stage. As she went over to Zoe, she saw that a red light on the amplifier was illuminated, indicating it was on. "But wouldn't he put his guitar back in the case when he was done and turn off the amplifier?" she asked.

"Definitely," Zoe answered. "This is expensive equipment. He'd never leave it lying around like this. And he'd lock the door after he left."

"He must have been interrupted," Nancy said. This time she couldn't stifle the bubble of worry rising up inside her. "I'm afraid something terrible has happened to Randy."

# 4

## Gone Without a Trace

Zoe looked around the Anchorage with haunted eyes. "Something must have happened to him," she said, slowly getting to her feet. "But what?"

"Let's take a look around. Maybe we'll find him," George said.

"Or at least some clue as to what happened to him," Nancy added.

While Bess and George looked around the rest of the room, Nancy and Zoe checked the stage itself. The other band members' instruments and amplifiers were all unplugged and stored neatly at the back of the stage. Other than Randy's guitar and amplifier having been left on, Nancy didn't see anything unusual.

"Nothing down here," Bess said a few minutes

later. "Should we check the room where the stuff for the auction is being stored?"

"Definitely," Zoe said. She was already halfway down the stairs, and Nancy was right behind her. When Zoe got to the room, she stopped so suddenly that Nancy almost rammed right into her.

"Oh, my gosh," Zoe whispered. "Look!"

Nancy glanced over Zoe's shoulder—then gasped. "The giraffe . . . It's been shattered!"

Chunks of green and yellow metal lay scattered on the floor. The giraffe's head was in two pieces, its eyes staring blankly into space. The two other jungle animals—the red gazelle and blue tiger—were leaning against the wall of the room.

"Oh, no!" Bess cried as she and George came into the room. "Who would do this?"

"Someone who doesn't want the Heights Gardens benefit to succeed," Nancy said. Hurrying over to the shattered giraffe, she bent over a sledge-hammer, which lay on the floor next to it. "This must be what the person used."

"Tim Chang?" George asked.

"He certainly has a motive," Nancy said. "Tim said last night that he hoped the benefit would flop. Maybe he thinks that if enough money *isn't* raised to renovate the Heights Gardens, people will reconsider his plan to build a theater." She frowned, remembering the cold glimmer in Tim's eyes as he'd glared at Randy the night before. "I think he overheard Randy talking about coming here last

31

night. He was definitely within hearing distance when Randy said he was going to work on his new song."

"Oh, yeah?" Zoe pressed her lips together, giving a tug to her wavy, dark hair. "You don't think Tim kidnapped him, do you? To make sure Randy won't be able to play at Friday night's concert?"

"No lead singer, no concert," George said. "That'd be extra insurance the benefit would fail."

The same thought had occurred to Nancy, but she also knew there were other possible explanations for Randy's disappearance. "Or Randy might simply have surprised the person who wrecked the giraffe," she said. "That would explain why the person didn't ruin more of the things for the auction. If Randy took him by surprise, he might not have had time to do any more damage."

"Thank goodness," Bess said. Her blue eyes played over the boxes and loose items that were scattered over the room. "But what should we do now? I mean, we still don't know where Randy is."

"We have to tell Mrs. O'Neill what happened," Zoe said. "She can lock up the Anchorage so no one else can get in. And we should call Randy's parents."

"Good idea," Nancy agreed. "Then we can decide whether or not to call the police."

When they reached the exit, Nancy took one last look around the Anchorage. She was about to pull open one of the double doors when a flash of luminous paint on the ground next to it caught her eye.

"Hey, look at this," she said. Bending down, she picked up a papier-mâché mask—a skeleton's face. "Look familiar?" she asked, holding it up for the others to see.

"I'll say," George answered. "That's one of the masks the Brooklyn Players were wearing last night."

Zoe took the mask from Nancy and turned it over in her hands. "So one of the actors *was* here," she said. "I bet it was Tim. And I bet he did something awful to Randy!"

"We still don't know that for sure," Nancy said. "Tim's not the only person around here who doesn't like Randy. Allison threatened Randy, too."

"And that guy we were working with yesterday, Vic, doesn't seem to like Randy very much, either," Bess added. "But I don't see what he or Allison would be doing with that mask."

"Or why they would smash the giraffe," Zoe said as she handed the mask back to Nancy.

Nancy took the mask and stowed it in her shoulder bag. She tried to make sense of all that had happened, but it was no use. "We're not going to learn anything by just standing around here," she said. "Come on, let's head back to the pier."

"Isn't that Ellis Island?" Bess asked Zoe and Nancy an hour later. The three of them were

33

looking out the windows lining the cabin of the Harbor Tours boat. George was in line at the snack bar at the rear of the cabin, waiting to get hot cocoa.

"Yes," Zoe answered. She gave a sigh, glancing halfheartedly at the complex of buildings and towers that made up Ellis Island. "I wish I could enjoy it more. But with Randy missing . . ."

"There's still a chance he'll turn up on his own," Nancy said. "Anyway, we've already done all we can. Randy's parents called the police. They can't even file an official report until he's been missing for two days. And we all agreed to wait at least until we get back to the pier before we do anything on our own to find him. Since we can't do anything except wait . . ."

"We might as well have a good time," Zoe finished. She rolled her eyes, then stared out the window at the blue-gray water that churned around the tour boat.

All around them, Bradley Prep students and the chaperons were clustered next to the windows. Battery Park and the twin towers of the World Trade Center rose up on the right. In the distance the Verrazano Bridge stretched across the water in graceful curving lines. But Nancy had the feeling that people were talking about Randy as much as they were looking at the sights. She'd heard his name dozens of times since the boat left the pier.

"Watch your backs," George said, coming up

with a cardboard box that held four steaming cups of cocoa. "Since we've got these to warm us up, maybe we should go out on the deck," she said, handing out the cups. "You know, smell the sea air, get the most of being out on the water . . ."

"Catch our death of cold," Bess added. "It's still winter, remember?"

"So?" George gave the others a challenging look, then reached for her parka from the pile stacked in a corner of the cabin.

"I'm with you, George. I could use some fresh air," Zoe said. "Peter, Nina, and Julio are already out there. Maybe they can help us think of what could have happened to Randy."

Looking through the cabin windows, Nancy saw the three band members and a few others at the bow of the boat. They were leaning against the railing, their faces red from the cold. It looked as if they were talking seriously among themselves.

"Come on, Bess," Nancy said, searching for her own parka. "We can come back in if we get too cold."

As soon as they got outside, a chilling wind hit Nancy's cheeks, sending her hair flying behind her. She could taste the salty spray in the air. Seagulls hovered overhead. Taking a sip of her hot cocoa, Nancy followed Zoe and George over to the others.

"I don't know what everyone is so upset about," she heard a guy say to Nina. At first all Nancy saw was the back of his parka. As she got closer and saw his face, she recognized Vic Wollenski's curly blond hair and chiseled face. "Randy's just being a typical rock and roller, totally irresponsible," Vic went on. "He's probably out on a joyride somewhere."

Next to Nancy, George shook her head in disgust. "Doesn't he realize that Randy could be in trouble?" she whispered in Nancy's ear.

All Nancy could do was shrug. "If he does realize it, he doesn't seem to care much," she whispered back.

"Not *all* rock musicians are irresponsible," Nina told Vic. "If Randy didn't show up this morning, it's because something happened to keep him from coming."

"*Not* because he's out partying," Julio added.

Zoe and Peter nodded, but Vic let out a snort. "All I know is that when I was counting on Randy, he turned around and stabbed me in the back."

"What's Vic talking about?" Bess whispered, shooting Zoe a questioning glance.

"It's a long story," Zoe told her, keeping her voice low. "About a year ago, Vic—"

"Hey! What's everyone doing freezing out here?" a voice called out from behind Nancy. She turned and saw Allison zipping up her jacket as she came out of the cabin. Ignoring everyone else, she walked over to Peter, Nina, and Julio. "You guys, I am *so* sorry about Randy," she said, and leaned against the railing next to them.

Nancy shot a surprised glance at Allison. Just the

36

day before, Allison had made it clear she hated Randy. Why the sudden concern for him?

Peter looked as if he was wondering the same thing. He glanced at Nina and Julio before he answered. "It's, uh, kind of a shock," he told Allison. "We're hoping that—"

"It's awful. But you know what they say—the show must go on," Allison cut in. She spoke in a pushy voice that rubbed Nancy the wrong way. "I just want you three to know that if Randy doesn't turn up by Friday, I'd be willing to fill in for him."

"I'm sure you would be," Vic said, rolling his eyes.

Allison blinked in surprise, then turned to face Vic. "What's that supposed to mean?" she asked.

"Now that Randy's missing, you can't wait to take his place," Vic said. He stuck his hands in his pockets and gave her a probing look. "You make it sound as if you *know* he won't be back by Friday. Makes me think maybe you know something the rest of us don't."

For the briefest second, Allison's eyes held a haunted, terrified expression. Then, just as quickly, it was gone. "I don't know what you're talking about!" she said hotly.

"Come off it, Allison," Vic scoffed. "Everyone in the Anchorage yesterday heard you say you'd make Randy pay for taking your place in the Lunatics!"

"You think I'd actually . . ." Allison's voice trailed off. She was so angry that she could barely talk. "You've got more of a reason to want to hurt

Randy than I do, Vic! Just get away from me, okay?"
Reaching out, she pressed both hands against Vic's chest and shoved.

Vic stumbled back a few steps before recovering his balance. "Hey!" he cried.

"Stop it, you two," Peter said as Vic took a step toward Allison.

Vic didn't appear to have heard him. Lashing back, he shoved Allison backward against the railing. He pushed her with such force that her feet lifted right off the deck.

"Help!" Allison cried.

Before Nancy could even think about moving, Allison flipped over the top of the railing.

# 5

# *Overboard*

"No!" Nancy yelled.

With lightning speed, she dived toward the railing. She hooked one arm firmly around the metal and threw out her other hand, trying to get hold of Allison, who was hanging on to the edge of the deck.

"I'm losing my grip!" she cried, her face white with fear.

Miraculously, Nancy's hand closed around Allison's jacket sleeve. Gritting her teeth, she gripped the nylon as tightly as she could. A split second later, Allison's fingers slipped from the deck.

"Whoa!" Nancy cried, as Allison's weight started to pull her over the railing, too. She felt someone grab her around the waist to anchor her.

"I've got you, Nan," George said.

Nancy had to use all her strength to hold on to Allison. "Help me pull her up!" she called out between clenched teeth.

"Hurry!" Allison squeaked out from below. Her face was completely white as she stared at the churning water below her.

Zoe, Peter, Bess, Nina, and Julio pitched in, and soon Allison was standing safely on deck.

"Are you all right?" Nina asked.

Allison managed a shaky nod. "Y-yes, but . . ." She looked past Nancy to where Vic was standing, slightly apart from the rest of the group. His hands were in his jacket pockets, and his eyes shifted moodily around. "You could have killed me."

The cabin door flew open and Mrs. O'Neill hurried outside. "What happened?" she asked.

Vic remained stonily silent while the others told Mrs. O'Neill how he had pushed Allison over the railing. As she listened, Mrs. O'Neill's face grew more and more serious. "How could you do such a thing?" she asked, turning to Vic.

"It was an accident. I didn't mean for her to go overboard," he said defensively.

"Are you trying to ruin everything?" Mrs. O'Neill asked, fixing him with a probing gaze. "The Heights Gardens benefit is very important. If people hear about stunts like this, it will only hurt our chances of raising enough money to fix up the park."

"Sorry, Mrs. O.," Vic told her. But his face remained stubborn and defiant.

"I want to talk to you and Allison inside," Mrs.

40

O'Neill said. "In fact, I'd like everyone in the cabin. We don't need any more accidents today."

As they went back inside, George leaned close to Nancy and whispered, "What's Vic's problem?"

Nancy shrugged. "What I'd really like to know is what he was talking about before, when he said Randy stabbed him in the back."

"I can tell you that," Zoe said. She threw her empty cup into the trash bin just inside the door. "About a year ago, Vic and some other kids decided to break into Bradley Prep gym at night. They weren't going to do anything serious, just decorate the basketball court with toilet paper."

"What does that have to do with Randy?" Bess asked.

"Randy was supposed to go with them, but at the last minute, his parents wouldn't let him go out," Zoe explained. "The trouble was, even though Randy didn't show up, the cops did."

"Uh-oh," George said.

Zoe nodded. "Vic was the only one who didn't get away. Somehow, Vic decided that Randy called the police and set them up. Randy didn't have anything to do with it, but Vic's hated him ever since."

"Do you think he finally decided to do something to get back at Randy?" Bess asked, biting her lip.

"Maybe," Zoe said. "But if Vic is the person who interrupted Randy at the Anchorage, then who destroyed the giraffe? Vic's been working hard for the Heights Gardens benefit. It doesn't make sense that he'd do something to sabotage the auction."

"He could have broken the giraffe so that we wouldn't suspect him," Nancy pointed out. "But I'm not ruling out Allison as a suspect, either. She seemed nervous when Vic accused her of knowing something about Randy's disappearance."

She glanced toward the other end of the cabin, where Mrs. O'Neill was still talking to Vic and Allison. "From now on," she said, "I'm going to keep an eye on both of them."

After the boat docked at the pier in Brooklyn Heights, the first thing Zoe did was call Randy's parents from the pay phone outside the Harbor Tours ticket office. She was frowning as she rejoined Nancy, Bess, and George at the edge of the pier nearest the street.

"No news?" Nancy guessed.

Zoe shook her head. "Mr. and Mrs. La Guardia still haven't heard a word from Randy," she answered. "They plan on searching the Anchorage themselves, but the police won't even start trying to find Randy until the day after tomorrow." She shoved her hands into her coat pockets, letting out her breath in a frustrated rush. "There's no way I can wait that long. What are we going to do!"

"Just because the police want to wait doesn't mean *we* have to," Nancy pointed out. She reached into her shoulder bag and exposed a corner of the skeleton mask they'd found in the Anchorage that morning. "I say we pay a visit to Tim Chang and find out what he knows about this."

"What about Vic and Allison?" Bess asked. "They both have reasons for wanting to get back at Randy. Shouldn't we keep an eye on them, too?"

George swiveled her head and looked at the groups of young people who were leaving the pier. "I don't see Vic. He must have left already. But there's Allison talking to Julio, Peter, and Nina again."

Allison and the three band members were standing on the pier next to the boat, Nancy saw. Allison seemed to be doing most of the talking. The other three looked as if they wished they were somewhere else. "I bet she's still trying to convince them to let her replace Randy at Friday's concert," Nancy said, shaking her head.

"Zoe! There you are," Mrs. O'Neill called brightly. She was standing next to the street, a few yards away. The other two chaperons were just getting into a car, but Mrs. O'Neill stayed behind. As she came over to Zoe, she patted the tote bag hanging from her shoulder and said, "I've brought everything we need to continue labeling items for the auction. Will all four of you be helping?"

Zoe looked blankly at Mrs. O'Neill for a moment. Then she blinked and tapped her forehead with the heel of her hand. "I totally forgot that I promised to help you this afternoon, Mrs. O.," she said. "I'm not sure I can. I mean, Randy's still missing, and—"

"Yes, of course," Mrs. O'Neill said right away. "I do hope nothing serious has happened to him. Do you have any idea at all where he could be?"

"Nothing concrete," Zoe answered. "Except that someone left that skeleton mask we told you about. We thought we'd go talk to Tim Chang and the Brooklyn Players now, to see if they know anything about it."

"Good idea," Mrs. O'Neill said with an approving nod. "Their theater is over on Montague Street—the Royale."

Bess gave Mrs. O'Neill an apologetic glance. "We hate to leave you in the lurch," she said, "especially now that the giraffe has been ruined. I mean, you'll have to call the police and stuff, won't you?"

"Not right away. I'm afraid any negative publicity will keep people away from the auction," Mrs. O'Neill said, frowning. "Anyway, you don't need to worry about that now. You've got more important things to do. Don't worry. Allison and I can take care of everything for the auction until you get back."

"Allison's helping you?" Nancy asked, instantly alert. When Mrs. O'Neill nodded, Nancy shot a meaningful glance at Zoe. "Maybe you *should* stay here and help out. George, Bess, and I can go to the theater on our own."

While you keep an eye on Allison, she added silently.

Zoe gave Nancy a quick nod to show that she understood. "Okay. You can meet me back at the Anchorage after you're done," she said. "Good luck!"

The Royale Theater was located in an old stone building that looked as if it had once been a church.

44

There were beautifully arched stained glass windows above the entrance and a stone turret.

"What a great building," George commented, gazing up at the turret. "No wonder Tim is upset about having to leave it."

"That doesn't justify wrecking an irreplaceable carousel giraffe," Bess said with a frown. "Or doing something to Randy so that he won't be able to play at the concert."

"*If* Tim is responsible. We haven't found that out for sure yet," Nancy reminded her.

Squaring her shoulders, she headed up the steps to the immense wooden entrance doors. As she was about to reach for the doorknob, the left door swung open. A man carrying a cardboard box angled out of the theater.

"Coming through," he said, as Nancy, Bess, and George jumped back to give him room. He went down the steps to a van parked in front.

"Excuse me," Nancy called to him. "Is Tim Chang around?"

The man hefted the box into the van. "In the main theater," he answered, without looking back.

"Thanks!" Nancy said. They went into a small foyer and through a curtained doorway into the theater. Rows of metal chairs were piled against the walls. The stage was empty, except for two piles of plush red fabric that looked like curtains. Tim was standing at the front of the stage in black jeans and a plaid flannel shirt. He was struggling to close the top of a cardboard box. Men and women came and went from the areas behind the stage, carrying more boxes.

"Looks like today's moving day," Nancy commented as she, Bess, and George went up to him.

Tim looked up at them and frowned. "We're not open to the public," he said curtly. His voice held the same commanding tone he'd used in the Heights Gardens the night before. "So, if you don't mind going out the same way you came—"

Nancy wasn't about to be brushed off so quickly. "Actually, we stopped by because we found something we think belongs to you," she said. Reaching into her shoulder bag, she pulled out the skeleton mask. "We found this inside the Anchorage this morning."

She watched Tim carefully for his reaction, but all he did was take the mask and toss it on top of the nearest pile of boxes. "Thanks," he said. He went back to taping the lid of the cardboard box.

Nancy exchanged curious looks with George and Bess. If Tim had had something to do with Randy's disappearance or the shattered giraffe, she would expect him to act shiftier—or at least a little uncomfortable. Instead, he was ignoring them completely!

"Um, Mr. Chang," George spoke up. "Were you in the Anchorage last night or this morning?"

When Tim looked up, he seemed surprised—and none too pleased—to find they were still there. "I've got better things to do than waste my time in the Anchorage," he scoffed. "In case you hadn't noticed, I'm busy taking apart my entire theater."

"If you weren't in the Anchorage, why did we find this mask there?" Bess asked.

Tim shrugged. "I really couldn't say." He waved to two young women who appeared from a hallway behind the stage. "Those boxes against the wall are next," he told them. "They need to go into the van before it leaves for RiteWay Storage."

Nancy saw the annoyed glimmer in George's eyes as Tim turned away from them again. "Look, Mr. Chang," George said, planting her hands on her hips. "In case *you* hadn't noticed, Randy La Guardia has been missing since last night. The last place anyone saw him was the Brooklyn Anchorage."

"Not my problem," Tim said. "As I said, I've got better things to worry about."

With that, he picked up the cardboard box he'd just taped shut and headed for the door.

"What a jerk!" Bess said as soon as he was gone. "He acts totally unconcerned about everything except his theater—even after hearing that Randy is missing."

"*Acted* is right," Nancy said. "Putting on an act is his profession, after all. Maybe he pretended he doesn't know anything about Randy's disappearance or that mask being found in the Anchorage. But . . ."

"Uh-oh. I recognize that look," George said, grinning. "What do you have up your sleeve, Nancy?"

Nancy pointed toward the stage. Hallways led back into the theater from either side of it. "As long

47

as we're here, we might as well take a look around," she said.

"Are you sure we should?" Bess asked, looking over her shoulder in the direction Tim had gone. "What if Tim catches us?"

"We'll have to make sure he doesn't," Nancy said. "Come on."

Taking the lead, she climbed the steps to the stage, then they darted into the hallway on the left without running into anyone. There were a few open rooms off the hall. As Nancy passed them, she saw that one held costumes. Two other rooms looked as if they were used for offices. There were people packing in all of them, but no one paid any attention to Nancy, Bess, and George.

"I haven't seen any place yet where Randy could be held captive," Nancy said, keeping her voice low. "With everything being emptied out, even the closets are wide open."

"Nancy, Bess . . . look!" George called softly.

She was standing in front of an open door at the end of the hall. Beyond it, dusty stairs spiraled upward and disappeared into the darkness of the turret.

"If Tim wanted to keep Randy in an out-of-the-way place until after the benefit, this could be it," Nancy said. She felt around inside the door, then grinned as her fingers found a light switch. When she flicked it on, a murky yellow light illuminated the stairs. "Come on!"

As she moved up the spiral staircase, the steps

creaked beneath her feet. A few times her hand brushed through a spider's web.

"Hurry," Bess whispered from behind her. "This place gives me the creeps."

Looking up, Nancy saw that the stairs ended at a wall that had a door set into it. "We're almost—"

Nancy broke off. At the bottom of the stairs, Tim was shouting, "Hey! Who left this door open? I told everyone to stay out of the tower."

Nancy, George, and Bess froze. Please don't come up here, Nancy begged silently.

Her hopes plummeted when she heard feet pounding toward them up the creaky stairs. Nancy saw the panicked expressions that Bess and George shot each other. She looked around, but there was nowhere they could go.

Seconds later Tim reached them. He stopped short. "What—"

The confused expression in his eyes quickly hardened to a cold, evil glare that chilled Nancy to the bone.

If looks could kill, she thought, George and Bess and I would be dead.

# 6

## Caught Red-handed

Nancy swallowed, frantically searching her mind for an explanation that would mollify Tim.

"We, uh . . . This is such a lovely old building," she finally said. She flashed him a smile she hoped was convincing, making up her story as she went along. "We couldn't resist taking a look around."

Tim's eyes narrowed to two dark slits. "Oh, yeah?" he asked in a voice filled with doubt. "You could get hurt wandering around by yourselves. This is an old building. Parts of it aren't safe."

"Maybe you could give us a tour?" Bess spoke up from behind Nancy.

Tim scowled. "I don't have time to entertain tourists," he said disdainfully. "I'm sorry, but you'll have to leave."

They followed him down the stairs and back

through the theater to the front doors. As soon as they stepped outside, Tim closed the doors firmly behind them.

"Wow," George said, flicking a thumb back toward the doors. "He's not about to win any prizes for friendliness, that's for sure."

Nancy nodded. "He certainly didn't want us snooping around in that tower," she said as they went down the steps into the cold, bright sunshine.

"Maybe he's more interested in being sneaky than nice," Bess said. "Do you think he's got Randy locked up there?"

"I don't know," Nancy admitted. "But even if Randy's there now, he probably won't be for long. The Brooklyn Players are moving out of the theater today, after all. Tim would have to move Randy someplace else."

George frowned, then snapped her fingers. "Didn't Tim say something about a storage place?"

"He did. RiteWay Storage," Nancy supplied. "Maybe we can find out where it is and check it out later. But for now, we'd better get back to the Anchorage and see how Zoe's doing."

They walked down Montague Street toward the East River, then followed the Promenade toward the Anchorage, admiring the view of the harbor. After about ten minutes, the Heights Gardens came into sight to their right, just across the street from the Promenade.

"Hey, isn't that Peter?" Bess asked, pointing toward the park. "Nina and Julio are there, too."

The three band members were sitting on one of

the run-down wooden benches near the pavilion, bundled up in jackets, hats, and scarves. They were holding take-out cups of hot cocoa and talking so intently they didn't notice Nancy, Bess, and George until they were right next to them.

"Hi." George greeted them with a smile. "You guys look so serious—like you're deciding the fate of the world or something."

Julio blinked at them in surprise, then smiled back. "Actually, we're deciding the fate of Friday's benefit concert," he explained.

"We have to think about what we're going to do if Randy doesn't turn up by then," Peter added soberly.

"He will," Nina said. She blew into her cup of cocoa before adding in a small voice, "At least, I hope so."

Nancy's heart went out to the three band members. She could tell they didn't want to believe anything bad had happened to Randy. She didn't want to believe it herself.

"We're doing everything we can to figure out what happened and where he is," Nancy said, trying to sound optimistic.

"Well, in the meantime, we've decided to accept Allison's offer to take Randy's place in Friday's concert," Peter said. He looked back and forth between Nina and Julio and let out a sigh. "We're not crazy about the idea. Allison's not nearly as talented as Randy."

"But if we don't find someone to play with us, we'll have to cancel the benefit," Julio said. "We can't let down all the people who've worked so hard to organize it."

He turned as a group of young people walked past the park, laughing and joking. "Hey, Sabrina!" Julio called out. "Have you seen Allison? We need to talk to her."

"Actually, she's at the—" Bess began, but she was interrupted by a brown-haired young woman who answered from the passing group.

"Who knows?" the young woman called back. "Allison's been totally unpredictable lately. Last night she was supposed to help us make a banner for the concert, but she left before we were even halfway done. Gave some excuse about having to do something important."

"Like maybe finding Randy at the Anchorage and doing something to make sure he wouldn't be able to play at Friday's benefit concert?" George whispered to Nancy as the group moved on.

Nancy nodded, thinking over the possibility. "Being in the Lunatics obviously means a lot to Allison," she said under her breath. "Maybe even enough to make her do something as desperate as abduct Randy."

But why would she wreck the giraffe? Nancy asked herself. That part still didn't make any sense. Besides, Nancy doubted Allison was strong enough. Shaking herself from her thoughts, she turned back to Peter, Nina, and Julio. "Allison's probably in the Anchorage. She and Zoe are helping Mrs. O'Neill label items for the auction," she told them.

"We're going there now, if you want to come along," Bess added.

"Sounds good." Nina drank the rest of her cocoa, then got to her feet and threw the empty cup into a litter basket. "We might as well get this over with."

"So, you guys finally came to your senses," Allison said a few minutes later.

Nancy, George, Bess, Julio, Nina, and Peter had arrived at the Anchorage to find Allison, Zoe, and Mrs. O'Neill taking a break. They were sitting cross-legged on the floor, munching potato chips and pretzels and drinking soda.

"Let's face it, you need me," Allison went on smugly. She jumped up from the floor and grinned at the band members. "Shouldn't we start practicing? I can get my guitar from home and be back here in twenty minutes."

"Great," Peter said, forcing a smile. "I guess we'd better get to work, then."

Allison started for the door, then hesitated. "You don't mind, do you, Mrs. O.?" she asked, turning an apologetic glance toward Mrs O'Neill.

"Heavens, no," Mrs. O'Neill said. She smiled at Nancy, Bess, and George. "These young ladies can help Zoe and me finish the labeling."

"Absolutely," Bess said.

"Thanks," Allison said. She grabbed her jacket and raced from the room. Peter, Julio, and Nina shrugged at each other before starting toward the doorway themselves.

"We might as well start setting up our equipment," Julio said.

Bess followed them to the doorway, shaking her head. "They don't seem excited about replacing Randy," she said softly. "Not that I blame them. It can't be easy to—"

Bess broke off suddenly and whipped her head around to look behind her. "Did you guys hear that?"

"Hear what?" George asked.

"Shhh!" Bess held a finger to her lips. She nodded toward the maze of tunnels that led deeper into the Anchorage, away from the entrance. "I thought I heard a voice coming from in there."

"Are you sure?" Nancy asked.

She and George were next to Bess in a flash. There were no lights past the room where the things for the auction were being stored. Nancy cocked her head to the side, staring into the murky darkness of the tunnels. At first she heard nothing but the sounds they all made breathing.

"I don't hear anything," Zoe whispered as she and Mrs. O'Neill came into the hall, too.

"It was probably your imagination," Mrs. O'Neill said. "These old tunnels are so mysterious, it's easy to imagine all kinds of sounds that aren't really there."

Nancy frowned. "You're probably right—"

She broke off with a gasp. This time she heard it—a faint voice calling from somewhere deep within the Anchorage tunnels.

"It's a cry for help!" she said.

# 7

## A Cry for Help

"Maybe it's Randy!" Zoe exclaimed. "Right here in the Anchorage!"

"Oh, I doubt it," Mrs. O'Neill said, shaking her head. "Mr. and Mrs. La Guardia were here a while ago and made a search of the tunnels, and they didn't find a thing."

"I know, but"—Zoe stared into the dark tunnels, her mouth pressed together in a determined line—"maybe they missed something."

"Your ears are playing tricks on you, that's all," Mrs. O'Neill insisted. "Besides, I can't let you go in there. It's too dark. You could get hurt."

"We can't just stand around and do nothing," George said, glancing at Mrs. O'Neill in disbelief. "Randy could be hurt!"

"George is right," Nancy said. She understood

56

Mrs. O'Neill's caution, but she couldn't stand the thought of waiting even another second to search for whoever had cried for help. "Isn't there a flashlight we could use?"

Zoe jumped back inside the room where they had been working. "I know I saw one somewhere," she murmured. She darted here and there, frantically searching, until she found a metal flashlight on a hook behind the door. "Come on!"

Zoe flicked on the flashlight and started down the dim hall, heading deeper inside the Anchorage. Nancy, Bess, and George kept close to her. Glancing over her shoulder, Nancy saw Mrs. O'Neill standing outside the room where the things for the auction were stored. She was frowning, looking after them with an expression Nancy couldn't quite read.

Then, all at once, Mrs. O'Neill hurried after them. "Oh, bother. I suppose I'd better come, too," she said. "Someone needs to make sure you don't get into trouble."

"Shh!" Zoe said, pressing a finger to her lips.

After about twenty feet, another tunnel branched off to the left. Nancy took a few steps into it and stood stock still, listening. A distant scraping noise echoed from somewhere down the dark tunnel. "This way! I think someone's down there," she whispered.

"Randy, is that you?" Zoe called. When no one answered, she said, "Hello? Is anyone there?"

"Oooooh," a voice echoed in the tunnels. "Help me . . ."

"It sounds like he's hurt!" Bess cried. "Hurry!"

Nancy didn't have to be told twice. She and Zoe ran down into the tunnel, with Bess, George, and Mrs. O'Neill close behind. They twisted left and right so many times that Nancy completely lost track of their route. Zoe's flashlight beam lit up spider webs, broken-down crates and planks of wood, and the dank stone walls of the tunnels. But Nancy still didn't see a person.

Then another moan echoed in the tunnels. This time it sounded as if it was coming from somewhere quite close. Nancy hurried past a chipped plank of plywood leaning against the stone wall. Just beyond it, the tunnel curved right. As she followed it around, the first thing she saw was a flashlight beam on the stone floor. A shadowy figure sat next to it. Zoe shone her own flashlight on the person, and the beam lit up curly blond hair and a muscular build.

"Vic!" Zoe exclaimed.

His face was twisted in pain, and he was clutching his ankle. "Ooooh," he moaned, as Zoe, Nancy, George, Bess, and Mrs. O'Neill rushed over to him.

"I know a little about first aid," George said. She bent over Vic's ankle, but he pulled it away from her.

"Here, let me," Mrs. O'Neill said. She dropped to her knees and pulled up the cuff of Vic's jeans leg. "Doesn't seem too bad," she murmured after gently probing for a moment. "What happened, Vic?" she asked. She looked worriedly over her shoulder. "What on earth are you doing back here?"

"I was, uh, just taking a look around," Vic said. "I always heard it was cool back here, so I decided to check it out. I guess I should have been more careful, though," he admitted. "The floor is so uneven that I twisted my ankle. I couldn't even move."

Vic's eyes shifted around uneasily. Nancy noticed that he didn't look anyone directly in the eye. She had a feeling there was something he wasn't telling them. But before she could ask him anything, Mrs. O'Neill spoke up. "These tunnels are nothing but trouble. I don't want you kids back here anymore," she said, grimacing into the dark stone corridor. "Now, let's get back to the main part of the Anchorage. You need to get home and ice your ankle, Vic. And make sure you see a doctor. The sooner, the better."

With Nancy, Zoe, Bess, and George helping to support him, Vic managed to limp back to the main room. He sat down heavily on the stairs leading up to the stage and propped his foot up next to him. While Mrs. O'Neill went outside to use a pay phone to call a cab, Nancy turned to Vic.

"Didn't it make you nervous to be in the tunnels all alone so soon after Randy disappeared from here?" she asked.

"Not really," he answered gruffly. "I don't know what everyone's worked up about. Randy's probably just out on a joyride."

Nancy looked at him closely. "You know, it's odd," she said slowly, "during the Harbor Tours cruise, you practically accused Allison of being responsible for Randy's disappearance. But now you're acting as if there's nothing to worry about at all." She fixed him with a probing stare before continuing. "I'm beginning to wonder if you're just trying to keep people from questioning whether *you* were involved."

"Me?" Vic shot her a hooded glance. "That's ridiculous."

"I don't know about that," Zoe put in. "You've been out to get Randy ever since you were caught in the gym last year."

Vic's pale blue eyes flashed angrily. He opened his mouth to say something, then clamped it shut again. Nancy had the feeling he was trying to get control over his emotions before he said anything. "That happened a long time ago," he finally told them. "Maybe I'm not about to volunteer to be Randy's best friend, but I'm not crazy enough to hurt the guy, either."

With that, Vic looked stonily away from them. Mrs. O'Neill returned from the phone soon afterward and helped Vic outside to wait for the taxi.

After the two had left, Zoe, Nancy, Bess, and George went back to the room where everything for the auction was. "What do you think? Is he telling the truth?" George asked as she reached for some tags and a pen.

"Beats me," Nancy admitted. "But Vic acted pretty shifty when Mrs. O'Neill asked what he was doing in the tunnels. I think he's hiding something."

"I don't know what, though," Zoe said. "Mrs. O'Neill was right about one thing. Randy's parents already made a search of the Anchorage. Mrs. O'Neill went with them herself. It doesn't seem possible that he could be here. The La Guardias even insisted on setting up a neighborhood watch here at the Anchorage. Different residents will stand guard each night to make sure nothing else is stolen or ruined."

"That sounds like a good idea," Bess said. "I just hope—"

"Good news," Mrs. O'Neill said brightly as she stepped into the room. "Another donation."

A young woman was right behind her, carrying a cardboard box. Her reddish brown hair was pulled back in a french braid, and freckles were sprinkled across her nose and cheeks.

"Just some stuff my dad had in the attic," the young woman said. "It used to belong to my great-grandfather."

"Really?" Mrs. O'Neill pulled open the cardboard flaps and bent over the box with interest. "Let's see what we have." She began gently sifting through the items. "Photos . . . newspaper clippings . . . Wonderful! These are from the

*Brooklyn Eagle.* That old newspaper died out in the 1950s," she said in a dreamy voice.

"Oh, these are a lot older than that. Great-granddad Donnelly was a police officer back before then," the young woman said. "All this stuff is from his private files on a case he worked on back in the '40s. He never did solve it. My father and granddad say he was totally obsessed with it."

Nancy stepped over to the box, looking over Mrs. O'Neill's shoulder. "An unsolved crime, huh? What was it?" she asked.

"Here she goes," George put in good-naturedly, flicking a thumb at Nancy. "One thing about Nancy Drew—she can never resist a good mystery."

"You get used to it after a while," Bess added with a grin.

Nancy laughed along with her friends, but she had to admit she was curious. "Do you mind if I take a look?" she asked Mrs. O'Neill.

Mrs. O'Neill's hazel eyes were glued to an article that lay on top of the pile. She was reading it so intently that she didn't even answer. Nancy glanced over her shoulder. The date at the top of the newspaper was July 21, 1941. Below it, a headline was splashed across the yellowed page in capital letters: "PRICELESS RUBY RING TAKEN IN DARING JEWELRY HEIST."

"Wow!" Nancy exclaimed. She skimmed the first paragraph. "According to this, a cat burglar struck a brownstone in Brooklyn Heights and made away with tons of jewelry," she murmured, "including a ruby ring worth hundreds of thousands of dollars."

"That's right," the woman who'd brought the box said. "The cops caught the cat burglar. Some guy called the Glove. My granddad said he had quite a reputation. He'd been stealing from wealthy Brooklyn Heights homes for years. Great-granddad Donnelly is the one who nabbed him somewhere out by Coney Island. He even recovered most of the jewelry."

"But not the ruby ring?" Nancy guessed.

The young woman shook her head. "The family who owned the ring kept it hidden in a doll in their safe. The police never found the doll or the ring, and the Glove never told what he'd done with them. When he died, I guess the secret of the ruby ring died with him." She gave a wave, then headed for the door. "Well, I've got to go now. See you!"

Nancy was so fascinated by the story that she barely waved goodbye. She tried to take another look at the pile of articles and photos, but Mrs. O'Neill was flipping through them so quickly that Nancy couldn't see them clearly.

"Unbelievable . . ." Mrs. O'Neill murmured. Her cheeks were flushed, and a faraway look was in her eyes. Shaking herself, she shot a sheepish glance at the others. "You'll have to excuse me. These old stories bring back a lot of memories," she said. She quickly replaced the items in their box and closed it, then took a deep breath. "We have a lot of work to do before Saturday's auction. It won't do to linger over each item that's donated."

Nancy wished she could curl up on a couch and read every single article Katie had brought, but she knew Mrs. O'Neill was right. "Anyway, we have an even bigger mystery to solve right now," she said, thinking out loud.

"Finding Randy," Zoe said.

Nancy nodded. She heard voices coming from the main room of the Anchorage. Seconds later guitar chords, drums, and an electric piano echoed in the air. As the group started to play, some of the chords didn't sound right to Nancy. But she reminded herself that it would take some practice before Allison got the music down.

"You guys, what are we going to do about finding Randy?" Zoe asked. Her brown eyes flickered from Nancy to Bess to George. "Did you find out anything from Tim Chang and the Brooklyn Players?"

Nancy, Bess, and George quickly told her about their visit to the theater. "If Tim did have something to do with Randy's disappearance, he didn't let on," Nancy finished. "But it's possible that he's got Randy stowed away somewhere, and that he's not going to let him go until after Friday's concert." She decided not to mention another possibility— that Randy was hurt . . . or worse.

"Still, I'd like to check out the storage place where the Brooklyn Players are keeping everything from their theater," Nancy went on. "And I wouldn't mind talking to the man who donated the giraffe. What was his name?"

Bess snapped her fingers a few times. "Mr. Eltman or—"

"Altman. Sammy Altman," Zoe supplied. "But why talk to him?"

"It seems strange that the giraffe is the only thing that was wrecked, that's all," Nancy said. "I'd like to find out how it fits into Randy's disappearance. If it does, that is." She turned to Mrs. O'Neill and asked, "Do you know where his secondhand store is? Didn't he say it's somewhere out in Coney Island?"

Mrs. O'Neill thought for a moment, her brow creased in concentration. "I'm not sure. . . ."

"We made a list of everyone who's donated things for the auction," Zoe put in. She hurried over to a table against the wall, where a notebook, tags, pens, and other supplies lay. "Here," she said, picking up the notebook. She flipped through the pages, then jabbed her finger at one of the ink entries. "Here! Sammy's Secondhand . . . He's on Mermaid Avenue. That's out at Coney Island, all right. Let's call him right now," she suggested. "Maybe we can make an appointment to see him tomorrow."

"So this is Coney Island," Bess said the following morning, as she, Zoe, Nancy, and George emerged from the subway station Wednesday morning.

Nancy paused on the sidewalk and looked around. They were on Surf Avenue, a wide boulevard lined with fast-food restaurants, secondhand stores, and stands where T-shirts and other tourist items were sold. Small alleys stretched back from Surf Avenue, leading to a boardwalk a few blocks away. Nancy saw an amusement park a block down Surf Avenue, but a chain-link gate covered the entrance. A towering Ferris wheel, roller coaster, and dozens of other rides stood empty. They looked as if they were waiting for people to come and fill them up.

"It's pretty deserted," George said, looking up and down Surf Avenue. "Even a lot of the stores are closed."

"In the winter there are mostly just locals around," Zoe said. "But when the weather warms up, Coney Island really comes alive. There are parades, tattoo artists, people everywhere you look . . ."

"One important place is open, anyway. There's Nathan's," said Bess. She pointed to a billboard sign across the street. Below the sign was a long, open counter with half a dozen vendors behind it. "They're supposed to have the best hot dogs in the world."

"We can sample them for ourselves in a little while," Zoe said with a laugh. "Our appointment with Mr. Altman isn't for another hour, but for now . . ." She patted the in-line skates that were slung over her shoulder. "Let's hit the boardwalk!"

Before Nancy, Bess, and George had left River Heights, Zoe had said they might want to bring their skates. Even though they took up a lot of room in her suitcase, Nancy was glad they'd have a chance to use them. Zoe led the way down a small alleyway called Schweikert's Walk, which ended up at the boardwalk.

"It's immense!" Bess exclaimed.

The boardwalk had to be almost a hundred feet wide. Diagonal wooden planks stretched as far as Nancy could see in both directions. Billboards, snack stands, and tacky souvenir shops lined one side of the boardwalk. Beyond the railing on the other side was a wide sandy beach and the choppy gray waters of the Atlantic. A long pier stretched out over the water to Nancy's right. A dozen or so people were dotted along the length of it, fishing.

"The cold isn't keeping people away from *here*," George said. She nodded to a pair of joggers who ran past, then sat down on a bench near the railing and began untying her sneakers. "This is going to be great!"

Within minutes Nancy, Bess, George, and Zoe were skating down the boardwalk. The cool sea breeze felt wonderful on Nancy's face, and the brisk exercise kept her warm. The boardwalk stretched on so far in front of them that Nancy felt as if they were on an endless wooden racetrack. It was so invigorating that for a moment she forgot all about Randy, the shattered giraffe, and all the unsettling events of the past few days.

"It looks as if there are lots of cool side streets around here," she commented. She nodded toward a ramp just ahead that sloped down to another alleyway leading back toward Surf Avenue.

"There are tons of funky old stores," Zoe said breathlessly. "After we skate the boardwalk, we can—"

Nancy didn't hear the rest of what Zoe said. A familiar figure standing in the alleyway had caught her attention. "You guys, I think I just saw Tim Chang!" she called out.

"You're kidding!" George said.

Nancy spun around in a U-turn and skated quickly back to the ramp. When she looked down the alleyway again, she saw that it *was* Tim. He was about halfway down the narrow street, leaning against the open doorway of a run-down building with boarded-up windows.

"What's he doing here?" George asked breathlessly, skating to a stop next to Nancy. Zoe and Bess were right behind her.

"I don't know," Nancy answered, "but—"

In that instant, Tim saw them. Even from down the block, Nancy saw his body stiffen with recognition. He glanced furtively left and right, and his face darkened into a frown. Then he whirled and disappeared inside the building, slamming the door behind him.

# 8

## Coney Island Intrigue

"What was that all about?" Bess wondered aloud.

"There's one way to find out," Nancy said. She shot her friends a challenging glance, then pushed off down the ramp on her in-line skates. "Let's follow him!"

Glancing over her shoulder, Nancy saw that Bess, George, and Zoe were all careening down the ramp behind her. It wasn't until she looked ahead of her again that Nancy saw about thirty gray-haired men and women in bathing suits coming toward them.

"Yikes!" she cried, skidding to the right to avoid hitting a robust-looking woman wearing sandals and a blue flowered suit with a terry cloth robe over it. "What . . . ?"

"It's a Polar Bear club," Zoe explained. "Believe

it or not, they actually go swimming in this weather."

"Voluntarily?" Bess asked, shivering inside her parka. "I don't believe it."

There were so many swimmers that Nancy lost sight of the doorway behind which Tim had disappeared. It was frustrating, but there was nothing to do except wait until they passed. "Excuse me," she said, trying to skate around a knot of men.

Finally, they burst around the other side of the group and sprinted to the doorway. To her relief, she saw that the door was ajar. A bit of gravel had lodged next to the frame, preventing the door from closing firmly. Nancy pulled the door open and skated inside.

She, Bess, Zoe, and George stopped just inside the door to catch their breath. Narrow beams of sunlight filtered through the spaces between the boards that were nailed over the windows. The half light was just enough to see they were in a large, empty room. Chunks of plaster had fallen from the walls, and there were gaps in the old wooden floor. Footprints in the dust led to a doorway at the far end of the room.

"He went that way," Nancy said, nodding toward the doorway. "Tim?" she called out tentatively.

Nancy could hear the sounds of footsteps somewhere inside the building. But if Tim had heard her, he didn't answer. She pushed forward on her skates, following the dusty prints.

70

"This place is very run-down," Bess spoke up, looking around nervously. "Be careful, Nan."

Nancy nodded and coasted gingerly across the creaky floor. She was afraid the boards might give way, but they held. She, Bess, Zoe, and George had just reached the hallway, when Nancy heard a door open and close somewhere ahead.

"There must be another way out of here," George said from behind Nancy.

Nancy picked up her pace, following Tim's footprints. They went down the hallway and through another open room to a foyer with double metal doors. Skating quickly to the doors, Nancy pushed them open. Bess, Zoe, and George were right behind her.

"Surf Avenue," Zoe said, looking left and right.

Nancy immediately recognized the strip of stores and burger joints. She scanned them, looking for Tim, then let out a sigh.

"He's gone," she said.

"Well," George said from the doorway, "we don't know for sure that Tim was doing anything wrong."

"Then why did he disappear so suddenly when he saw us?" Zoe asked. She looked at Nancy, Bess, and George. "What if he abducted Randy and this is where he's keeping him?"

Nancy looked back over her shoulder. "I don't see any footprints besides the ones we just followed. Randy definitely wasn't in any of those rooms," she said. "Still, I guess it can't hurt to take a look around." She shrugged off her backpack, then unzipped it and pulled out her sneakers. "After I take off my skates."

It took about ten minutes to check the two-story building. All they found were empty offices. Except for Tim's footprints downstairs, there was no sign anyone had used the building in a long time. As they stepped outside onto Surf Avenue, Zoe gave Nancy, Bess, and George a weak smile. "Thanks for checking, anyway," she told them.

"No problem. I just wish we were having better luck finding out what happened to Randy," Bess said, "and who's trying to ruin the Heights Gardens benefit."

"Maybe Mr. Altman will be able to help us," Nancy said. "We're supposed to meet him in just twenty minutes."

"Which leaves us just enough time," Bess said.

"For what?" Nancy, George, and Zoe all asked at once.

Bess grinned at them. "Nathan's hot dogs, what else?"

Mr. Altman's store was just a block away from Surf Avenue. A sign above the entrance read Sammy's Secondhand. As Nancy, Zoe, Bess, and George walked toward it, Nancy saw that the dusty storefront window was filled with old bicycles, radios, and furniture.

"This is the place," Zoe announced. She pulled open the door, and a small bell jingled overhead.

The store wasn't wide, but it stretched back over

fifty feet. A scarred wooden counter stood near the door, with an old-fashioned black metal cash register on it. The rest of the store was filled with furniture, audio equipment, clothing—even statues and park benches. Mr. Altman was sitting on the floor in front of a jukebox that looked as if it belonged in a 1950s diner. The front panel was open, and he was tinkering inside with a screwdriver. He looked up, then blinked in surprise.

"Eleven-thirty already, eh?" he said, a warm smile spreading across his face. He got to his feet, wiped his hands on his flannel shirt, and came toward the front of the store. On the way, he stopped to pick up a stack of chrome-and-vinyl stools, which he lined up in front of the counter. "You can make yourselves comfortable on these."

"Thanks. It looks like you have a lot of great stuff here," Bess said, shrugging off her parka and looking around. "I bet someone could poke around for weeks and still not see everything."

"Sometimes I myself forget all the things I have here," Mr. Altman answered with a chuckle. "That's one of the reasons I decided to donate those carousel animals for the Heights Gardens auction. I figured it couldn't hurt to clear out this place some."

Even without the carousel animals, Sammy's Secondhand seemed stuffed to the gills. But Nancy loved the comfortable, homey feel of the place. "About the carousel animals . . ." she began as she climbed onto one of the stools.

"When Zoe called, she mentioned that the

73

giraffe was broken and that your friend is missing," Mr. Altman said, frowning. He sat down behind the counter.

"Anything you can tell us about the carousel animals might help," Nancy added. "Where you got them, that kind of thing . . ."

Mr. Altman ran a hand through his thinning dark hair, thinking for a moment. "Those cast-iron creatures have been in the store ever since I can remember," he began. "My grandfather must have gotten them from the wreck of the fire that destroyed the Jungle Carousel back in 1941."

"Fires were a big danger out here at Coney Island in those days, weren't they?" Zoe asked.

"Oh, yes," Mr. Altman said, nodding. "The amusement parks were infamous firetraps. The old Steeplechase Park burned to the ground in 1907. Dreamland went up in smoke in 1911. And in July of '41 came the big fire that took the Seafoam Palace—that's where the Jungle Carousel was."

George gave him an impressed nod, shifting her weight on her stool. "You really know a lot about Brooklyn history," she said.

"It's easy when you live in a place as fascinating as Coney Island," Mr. Altman said.

Nancy only half listened to his last words. She was still mulling over the dates of the fires Mr. Altman had mentioned. "July of 1941, huh?" she echoed, thinking out loud. It took her a moment to remember why the date sounded familiar. "That's when that theft took place, isn't it? The one where the Glove stole that ruby ring?"

She didn't even realize she'd spoken aloud until she saw the look of surprise on Mr. Altman's face. "Now, how do you know about the Glove?" he asked.

"Someone brought in clippings from the case," Zoe explained.

Nancy gave a sheepish smile. "Sorry. The ruby ring doesn't have anything to do with why we came here," she said. "Is there anything else you can tell us about the carousel animals, Mr. Altman? Can you think of anyone who's shown special interest in them lately?"

Mr. Altman thought for a moment, then shook his head. "They're unusual novelty items, but they were buried in the back room for years. No one's ever asked about them that I remember," he answered.

"Just a while ago we saw someone near here who might have had something to do with the sabotage and Randy's disappearance," George put in. She described Tim, then asked, "Maybe *he's* been in your store?"

Again Mr. Altman shook his head. When Nancy described Allison, he didn't recognize her, either. "Sorry," he said. "I wish I could be more helpful."

"You *have* been a help," Nancy assured him. "Since it doesn't seem as if anyone has shown special interest in the carousel animals, maybe the sabotage was random. It looks like whoever broke the giraffe did it simply to ruin the benefit and not because of anything special about the giraffe itself."

She, Zoe, Bess, and George thanked Mr. Altman, then put on their jackets. "It was fun hearing about the old amusement parks," Bess commented as they headed for the door. "They must have been amazing. I mean, wouldn't you love to go back in time so we could ride on the Jungle Carousel when Seafoam Palace was still around?"

"I'll bet it was something to see," Mr. Altman said. "Unfortunately, all that's left of it now are photographs. I donated one for the auction, as a matter of fact."

"Really?" Zoe asked. "Maybe we can take a look at it when we get back to the Anchorage."

The phone on the counter rang, and Mr. Altman reached out and picked up the receiver. "Hello?" he said. "Yes, she's here. Hold on." He held out the receiver to Zoe. "It's for you."

"I wonder who . . . ?" Zoe shot Nancy, Bess, and George a curious look as she took the phone from Mr. Altman. "Hello? Oh, hi, Peter. What's up?"

As Zoe listened, her face drained of color. "Oh, no," she gasped. "This is awful!"

"What's awful?" Bess asked. "What happened?"

"Hang on a sec, Peter." Zoe cupped a hand over the receiver, shooting Nancy a bleak glance. "The cast-iron tiger from the Jungle Carousel," she said, her voice barely above a whisper. "Someone's destroyed it."

76

# 9

## Endangered Animals

"I can't believe someone wrecked that beautiful old tiger," Bess said an hour later. "What a shame."

Nancy couldn't agree more. She, Bess, George, and Zoe had just returned to the Anchorage from Coney Island. They'd found Mrs. O'Neill, Peter, Julio, and Nina in the room where the auction items were being stored. Pieces of the blue-glazed tiger were strewn across the floor in front of them. Mrs. O'Neill was on her hands and knees, sifting through the broken bits of molded cast iron.

"What happened exactly, Mrs. O'Neill?" Nancy asked. "Was anyone else here when you arrived?"

Mrs. O'Neill sat back heavily on her heels and brushed the dust off her gloves. "There's not much to tell, really," she said. "John Ward was still here when I arrived. I didn't look closely, but I'm sure the tiger was still intact."

"John Ward? Is he part of the neighborhood watch that Mr. and Mrs. La Guardia set up?" George asked.

"Yes," Mrs. O'Neill told her. "He'd been cooped up in here for hours, so I walked outside with him and we chatted for a while. We were right next to the door—I don't see how anyone could have gotten inside. But when I came back here, I found this." With a sweep of her gloved hand, she gestured toward the broken pieces of cast-iron tiger at her feet.

"We must have gotten here right after that," Julio added. He leaned against a table covered with framed photographs, all labeled for the auction. "Mrs. O. was picking through the wrecked pieces. She looked so upset that she didn't even see us at first. Peter remembered you saying yesterday that you were going to some secondhand store out at Coney Island, Zoe. We tracked you down there."

George stepped over to the far end of the room, where the red cast-iron gazelle leaned against the wall. "Now there's only one Jungle Carousel animal left," she said quietly. "I hope nothing happens to this poor creature, too."

"It's a beautiful shade of red," Bess said, "almost like a ruby."

"It's weird. Out of all the things in here . . ." Zoe

gestured to the auction items with a sweep of her hand. "Why choose only the carousel animals to destroy?"

Nancy had been wondering the same thing. "Well," she began, thinking it out for herself, "if someone wants to make sure the auction doesn't earn much money, it makes sense they'd try to destroy the most expensive items."

"And the jungle animals *are* unusual," Bess said, picking up on Nancy's thoughts. "I'll bet the giraffe and tiger would have brought high prices at the auction. Especially if they were sold as a set with the gazelle."

"Mmm," said Nancy. "Of course, there are a lot of other things here that look valuable, too. What about the Brooklyn Dodgers jersey? Or some of the this antique furniture?" she asked. "And how did someone get in here, with Mrs. O'Neill standing right outside? The person couldn't have just materialized out of thin air."

No one had any answers for her—not that Nancy expected them to. Still, she couldn't squelch the feeling that there was something she was missing. If only she could put her finger on what it was. . . .

"Hello!" Allison's voice called from the main room, breaking into Nancy's thoughts. "Peter? Julio? Nina? Where *is* everyone?"

Seconds later, Allison appeared in the doorway. Her cheeks were red, and her short blond hair had a flyaway look, as if she'd been running. "Here you all are," she announced, as if she'd just made an important discovery. "What's going on? Aren't we supposed to be practicing?"

"You were supposed to meet us here at noon, Allison," Peter said, glancing at his watch. "You're over an hour late."

"I, uh . . . Something came up," Allison said. Nancy didn't miss the way her eyes flitted nervously around the room. "But I'm ready now."

"Come on. Let's set up," Julio said. "We're supposed to meet a Roz Townsend from the *Brooklyn Heights Bugle* on the Promenade at two. We have to hustle if we want to rehearse *and* make it to the interview on time."

Allison's eyes lit up. "A newspaper interview? That's great!"

"Oh, my." Mrs. O'Neill looked up suddenly after Allison, Peter, Julio, and Nina had left the room. "I was supposed to meet my husband for lunch fifteen minutes ago. He could use some cheering up, goodness knows. It's been hard for him since he got laid off."

"Oh—I'm sorry," Bess said.

"It's certainly not your fault," Mrs. O'Neill said. "Businesses are all cutting back. Bill just happens to be one of the latest casualties. Losing the income is bad enough, but I think the hardest thing for him to adjust to is being idle during the day. He's simply not used to it."

Nancy felt bad for Mr. O'Neill. Losing his job had to be tough.

"I hope he'll find another job soon," Mrs. O'Neill went on. "In the meantime, he's been helping out with the benefit. He was going to stop by the printer and pick up more posters before meeting me for lunch."

"Maybe we should come with you to get them," Zoe said. "That way, we can start putting them up right away."

"That's the spirit," Mrs. O'Neill said. "The cafe's just a few blocks away, on Henry Street."

The Cranberry Cafe had some of the most delectable-looking desserts in the window that Nancy had ever seen. Inside were round tables and a copper coffee bar with an espresso machine on it. The smells of coffee and pastries filled the air.

"Margaret Kennedy O'Neill, where have you been?" a man with thinning gray hair called from a rear table. "I've been waiting an eternity!" He was dressed in slacks and a shirt and vest. His overcoat was folded over the back of his chair. A package wrapped in brown paper rested on the table in front of him.

"Sorry. We had an emergency," Mrs. O'Neill told him. She bent to give him a kiss on the cheek, then introduced Zoe, Nancy, Bess, and George.

"Pleased to meet you," Mr. O'Neill said. He smiled, but Nancy noticed the worry lines around his eyes and mouth. "Here are the posters," he added, nodding at the package on the table.

"Thanks," Zoe said as she scooped it up. She started to turn away, then stopped herself. "By the

81

way, when we were talking to Mr. Altman, he mentioned that he donated a photograph of the Jungle Carousel for the auction. But I don't remember labeling it or seeing it around. Do you know where it is, Mrs. O.?"

Mrs. O'Neill thought for a moment. "I *do* remember taking it out of the box on Monday," she said. "But to be honest, I haven't seen it since."

Bess shot a worried look at Nancy. "You don't think—"

"That someone took the photograph, too?" Nancy finished. "Maybe. But what I still don't understand is, what's so important about that particular carousel?"

Nancy let out a sigh, pushing her reddish blond hair from her face. It had been a day and a half since Randy had disappeared and the giraffe was shattered. If they didn't find out soon who was responsible, Nancy was afraid they might never see Randy alive again.

"Where should we put up the posters?" Nancy asked Zoe half an hour later. They had just arrived at the Promenade, along with Bess, George, and several other students from Bradley Prep whom they'd picked up at the Anchorage.

"Let's see . . ." Zoe looked up and down the Promenade as she handed out posters and rolls of masking tape from a canvas bag on the ground next to her. "Let's tape them to every lamppost along here. Lots of people come to the Promenade to run and walk their dogs. We want to make sure they all know about the benefit."

As Nancy followed Zoe's gaze, she caught sight of a familiar person who was just coming onto the Promenade. "There's Vic," she said. His hands were in his pockets, and he sauntered easily along. "He seems to have made a miraculous recovery, considering that he sprained his ankle a few hours ago."

She waved at him. "Vic! How's your ankle?" she called out.

Vic's eyes narrowed slightly when he saw them. He hesitated, then walked slowly over to them. "I guess it wasn't so serious, after all," he said. "I put some ice on it, and it felt much better." He rotated his foot, as if to prove his words. But there was something about the shifty way he looked around that Nancy didn't trust. She caught the doubtful looks George, Bess, and Zoe shot each other, too.

"Well, if you're feeling okay, you're just in time to help us," Zoe said, holding out some posters and a roll of tape to Vic.

Vic started to shake his head, then seemed to think the better of it. "Okay," he told them. He took the posters and tape, then walked toward the closest lamppost.

"No one gets over a sprained ankle that fast," George said, raising an eyebrow. "I mean, he couldn't even walk when we found him. Makes you wonder if he made the whole thing up, doesn't it?"

"But if he was sneaking around in the Anchorage, why would he pretend to hurt himself and call everyone's attention to what he was doing?" Zoe asked.

Nancy didn't know, but she still felt sure that Vic was up to something.

"Hey, look," Bess said, nodding farther down the Promenade. "I guess the Raving Lunatics weren't late for their interview, after all."

Nina, Julio, and Peter were leaning against the Promenade railing, with the Manhattan skyline behind them. A reporter holding a tape recorder was interviewing them while a photographer snapped pictures. Allison was sitting several yards away on a park bench. Her arms were crossed over the front of her jacket, and the expression on her face was anything but happy. When she saw Zoe and her other classmates, she got up and walked over to them.

"I don't know why I offered to bail them out by playing at the benefit," she grumbled, shooting an annoyed glance over her shoulder. "Peter, Julio, and Nina decided not to include me in the interview. Roz Townsend is taping."

"Well, you're not officially part of the band," George said slowly.

"Besides, there's still a chance that Randy will turn up before the concert," Zoe added. "He's the biggest reason for the Lunatics' success. The rest of the band may be afraid they won't get a good crowd if they tell Roz Townsend Randy might not be there."

Nancy heard someone snort behind her. She turned and saw Vic walking past them with his posters and tape. He stopped and gave Allison a challenging glance. "Stop acting as if you're doing everyone a favor," he told her. "The only thing you're concerned about is elbowing your way back into the Lunatics. You don't care about Randy or the benefit."

"What?" Allison turned to face Vic, her eyes flashing with anger. "I don't have to put up with your insults."

Nancy didn't want to see a repeat of the fight the two had had during the Harbor Tours cruise. She stepped between the two, grabbed Allison's arm, and steered her smoothly away from Vic. "Allison! Can you help me put up these posters?" she asked.

"I, uh . . ." Allison glared at Vic. Then, she let out her breath and grabbed the posters Nancy held out. "Sure. Anything to get away from him."

Bess, Zoe, and George clustered around Nancy and Allison, and they steered Allison toward the next lamppost. Looking over her shoulder, Nancy saw Vic shake his head in disgust, then walk the other way.

"I love the old buildings around here," Bess said, looking at the row of brownstone houses along the Promenade. Nancy could tell she was trying to keep Allison distracted. "They've got such a feeling of history."

"That's one of the reasons it's so important to save the Heights Gardens, so that we don't lose the special atmosphere this neighborhood has," Zoe said. She put her canvas bag on the ground, then reached in to get a poster. "Lots of famous writers lived in Brooklyn Heights. Walt Whitman, Truman Capote, Thomas Wolfe, Marianne Moore."

"Don't forget about the *in*famous people who've been here, too," George said, raising an eyebrow. "Who knows? We could be looking right at the brownstone the Glove robbed back in 1941."

"The Glove?" Allison echoed, looking at George in confusion. "What's that?"

"The Glove is a *who*," Bess answered, laughing. "A cat burglar."

She, Nancy, George, and Zoe took turns telling Allison about the robbery they'd read about and the ruby ring that was never recovered. "The ring was worth several hundred thousand dollars even back then," Zoe finished. "It would probably be priceless today."

Nancy turned as someone let out a low whistle behind them. She frowned when she saw that Vic was there once again. He was kneeling next to Zoe's canvas bag. Nancy shot a worried glance at Allison. To her relief, Allison ignored Vic completely. She, Zoe, George, and Bess were already making their way farther along the Promenade.

"A priceless ruby ring, huh?" He pulled some posters from Zoe's bag, then looked up at Nancy with gleaming eyes. "No one ever found it?" When Nancy nodded, he asked, "When did you say it was stolen?"

"In 1941," Nancy told him. "Just a few days before a big fire out at Coney Island. That's when the Jungle Carousel was destroyed, as a matter of fact."

Vic shot her a funny look, then stood up. "Well, if no one's found it yet, it's probably gone for good." Rolling up the posters in his hand, he walked away.

Nancy picked up Zoe's canvas bag and followed Zoe, Bess, George, and Allison. "I keep thinking about the coincidence," she said when she caught up to them, "that the Glove stole the ruby ring just days before the carousel was destroyed in that fire."

"I don't see how the two things could be connected," George said, with a shrug. "They just happened to take place at about the same time, that's all."

Nancy reached into the canvas bag for another poster. "You're probably right, I'm just being—"

She broke off, blinking at the piece of paper she'd pulled from the bag. "Hey, this isn't a poster," she said. "It's a note!"

"You're kidding!" said Bess. "What does it say?"

Nancy held out the paper, which said: "If you want to know where Randy is, meet me tonight at the carousel in Prospect Park, 10 P.M."

# 10

## Rendezvous at the Carousel

"It's about Randy!" Zoe gasped. She whipped her head left and right, looking up and down the walk. "But who left it?"

Nancy shrugged. Students were scattered all across the Promenade, putting up posters. "Anyone," she admitted. "Lots of people have stopped by for posters and tape. It's not as if we were holding the bag every second."

"Vic was digging around in the bag a second ago," George said. "Maybe he put the note in there."

Zoe frowned toward Vic, who was taping a poster to a lamppost about fifty feet away. "What a snake," she said. "I bet it *was* him."

"We don't know that for sure," Nancy said.

"After all, he's not the only one who could have been involved in Randy's disappearance."

She shot a sideways glance at Allison, but she didn't appear to have heard Nancy. Allison was still staring at the note. Her face was white, her blue eyes wide with fear.

"Um, Allison? Do you know anything about this?" Nancy asked, waving the note.

Allison blinked. "No. W-why would I?"

Good question, Nancy thought. She remembered what Allison's classmate Sabrina had said the day before, about Allison suddenly leaving the poster-making party the night Randy disappeared. And that very morning, right after the blue carousel tiger had been smashed, Allison had acted edgy when Peter asked why she was late for practice. Nancy couldn't ignore the possibility that Allison knew more about Randy's disappearance—and the smashed carousel animals—than she was letting on.

"You seem really busy these days, Allison," Nancy said, without answering Allison's question. "First you skip out on making a poster for the Heights Gardens benefit on Monday night. Then you're late to rehearse with the Raving Lunatics today."

Allison looked around uneasily, brushing a hand through her short, blond hair. "It's nothing to make a big deal about," she said. "What I do with my own time isn't anyone's business but mine."

Peter, Julio, and Nina strolled by with Roz Townsend, the reporter from the *Brooklyn Heights Bugle*. They were talking easily while the photographer caught everything on film.

"Tell me something," Ms. Townsend was saying. "Is there any truth to the rumor we've heard that Randy La Guardia won't be playing at the Heights Gardens benefit concert?"

Nancy saw the uncomfortable looks that flashed among Nina, Peter, and Julio. "Well, even though Randy wasn't able to make it for this interview, we're hopeful that he'll be available to play at the concert," Peter said.

"Does that mean he *isn't* missing?" the reporter pressed. "An anonymous caller told us he'll be replaced by a new singer." The woman flipped back a few pages in the small notepad she carried. "Ms. . . ."

"Demar!" Allison spoke up. She strode over to the reporter, a huge smile on her face. "Allison Demar. I'm pleased to meet you."

"There is a slight chance that Allison will play with us," Peter said quickly. "Nothing's definite yet."

He, Julio, and Nina were all frowning at Allison, but Allison didn't seem to notice. She followed along, talking happily to the reporter as the group continued down the Promenade.

"An anonymous source, eh?" George said dryly. "I bet Allison called in that information herself."

"Probably," Nancy agreed. "That doesn't mean she's responsible for Randy's disappearance. But she did act awfully edgy when I asked her about Monday night."

"Maybe *she* left that note about Randy," Bess suggested.

Zoe frowned as Allison posed for the photographer up ahead. "As Nancy said, there's no way to be sure. But I guess we have something to be glad about," she said. "If whoever wrote that note knows where Randy is, that at least means he's alive, right?"

"I hope so," Nancy answered. She glanced at the note again, tapping it lightly. "I wonder why the person wants to meet at a carousel? I mean, the only items for the auction that have been wrecked so far are the giraffe and tiger from the Jungle Carousel."

"Do you think there's any connection?" George asked.

"I don't know," Nancy said, "but I'm sure of one thing. At ten o'clock tonight I'm going to be at the carousel in Prospect Park . . . wherever that is."

"It's just a few subway stops from here," Zoe told her. "Prospect Park is huge—even bigger than Central Park, in Manhattan. It's got lawns, old pavilions, lakes, a boathouse, woods. The carousel is near the northern edge of the park. It's a beautiful spot, but"—she bit her lip, looking nervous—"it's not open at night. It's bound to be deserted."

"What if it's a trap?" Bess asked.

"That's a chance I'll have to take," Nancy said firmly. "You guys don't have to come if—"

"We're definitely going with you," George said. "There's no way we'll let you meet some creep in the middle of nowhere at night."

"I've got an idea," Zoe said, and snapped her fingers. "The carousel isn't far from the Picnic House. That's this cool brick building where they give lectures and concerts and stuff. I bet Mrs. O'Neill could arrange for the Lunatics to practice there tonight. She's pretty active in the parks association."

Bess nodded eagerly. "That'd be great," she said. "That way, if anything happens, at least help won't be far away."

"Sounds good," Nancy agreed, grinning at her friends. "Let's do it!"

It was dark when Nancy, Bess, George, and Zoe arrived at Prospect Park Wednesday evening. A low stone wall surrounded the park, broken by entrances every few blocks. Paths leading into the park were lit by old-fashioned cast-iron lamps.

"The Picnic House is this way," Zoe said. She led the way down a path that wound around the administration building and across a road. There, on top of a small hill, was an elegant brick building with a slate roof sloping up sharply into the black night sky. Light spilled out of the wide picture windows wrapped around it.

Zoe led them inside. They were in a large open room. The Raving Lunatics were playing at the far end of it while half a dozen teenagers looked on.

"That's 'Gravity to Go-Go,'" George whispered, tapping her foot to the catchy beat. Allison was singing and playing lead guitar. Even though she seemed to be putting all her energy into the music, the song didn't sound nearly as rich as Nancy remembered it.

"They're okay," Bess said slowly, "but without Randy . . ."

"The music is missing something," Zoe said. She let out a sigh, shaking her head. "I just wish I knew where Randy is," she said in a small voice.

"I hope we'll find out soon," Nancy said. She went over to a set of glass doors set into the wall opposite the entrance. They opened onto a balcony that overlooked the park.

"The carousel is that way," Zoe said, pointing as she came up next to Nancy. "Over to the left." Nancy could make out a path that wound around a huge open lawn before disappearing into the pitch-black woods to the north. "We can follow that path through the woods, but I think it will be safer to take the street that runs just outside the park."

"Where we just were?" Nancy asked.

Zoe nodded. "The street goes to the north side of Prospect Park. From there, another path leads just inside the park to the carousel."

Nancy checked her watch, then took a deep breath. "We might as well get going," she said.

"You were right, Zoe," Bess whispered, twenty minutes later. "It *is* deserted around here."

She, Nancy, Zoe, and George had just turned into the park from the street at the northern edge. The turn-of-the-century lamps cast an eerie glow down the path. Their feet crunched on the gravel, echoing into the night. Zoe held a flashlight, which she flicked toward the trees and shrubs around them.

"The carousel is to the right," Zoe said, swinging her flashlight beam in that direction.

The gravel path curved around to a looming dark shadow. As Zoe's beam flickered over the structure, Nancy saw that it was an octagonal building. Arched openings in each side of the building were covered by metal bars, and she could see fanciful carousel horses inside.

George peered into the shadows surrounding the building. "I don't see anyone," she whispered.

"Neither do I." Nancy cocked her head to one side, but all she heard was the sound of their own breathing.

"Maybe we should wait at those benches," Bess whispered in a shaky voice. She pointed to two long wooden seats under a lamp. "At least they're not in the pitch black."

Nancy hit the button on her watch to light up the

time. "It's a few minutes before ten," she said. "Whoever left that note still has—"

"Shhh!" George hissed. She stopped suddenly and stared into the woods to their left. "Did you hear that?"

Nancy froze, listening. She heard footsteps rustling through the leaves. They were coming from the wooded area next to the carousel. "Someone's in there," she whispered. "Hello?" she called.

There was no answer. Zoe moved her flashlight beam slowly over the surrounding area, but all Nancy saw were trees and bushes.

"Maybe it's an animal?" Bess whispered.

"It sounded like a person to me," Nancy whispered back, frowning into the darkness. "Wait— there it is again!" She started toward the woods to her left. "I can't tell exactly how far away the person is. Maybe we should split up and angle in from different directions."

Zoe, Bess, and George nodded. While Nancy went straight into the woods, they fanned out on either side of her. She could see their silhouettes going deeper into the brush and Zoe's flashlight beam flickering over the leaves, trees, and grass. Nancy took one slow step at a time, trying not to make too much noise. Somewhere ahead, she again heard the rustling of feet in the leaves.

"Hello? Are you the—"

She heard another pair of footsteps crashing through the brush from the direction of the carousel. They were coming from behind, heading straight for her!

"Who . . . ?" Nancy whirled, blinking into the darkness. "Bess? George? Zoe? Is that . . ."

She caught a fleeting glimpse of a hulking shadow charging toward her. A split second later, she felt a painful blow to the side of her head. The last thing she remembered was the jellylike feeling in her legs as she slipped senselessly to the ground.

# 11

## A Close Call

"Nancy, are you all right?" Zoe's voice floated toward Nancy in a dreamy, dark fog.

"Ooooh," Nancy groaned, and slowly opened her eyes, then winced as Zoe's flashlight beam shone in her face. The side of her head throbbed. Zoe, Bess, and George were clustered around her. Even in the darkness, Nancy could see the worried looks on their faces.

"I guess I'm okay," she said groggily. It took her a moment to realize she was lying on the ground in the woods near the Prospect Park Carousel. As she gingerly pushed herself up to sit, it came back to her—the shadow lunging for her just before she passed out.

"Someone attacked you," George said grimly. She pointed to a rock the size of a fist, which lay on the ground next to Nancy. "This must be what the person used."

"We heard you shout. But by the time we got here, whoever knocked you out was gone," Bess added.

Nancy frowned, thinking back over the moments before she lost consciousness. "You guys, I'm pretty sure there were two people out here tonight besides us," she said. "We were following one person, but whoever attacked me came from a different direction."

"Really?" George asked. "But the note we found said, 'Meet *me* at the carousel.' That sounds as if only one person planned to be here."

"Maybe whoever wrote the note is in cahoots with someone else," Nancy said, thinking out loud. "They could be working together to ruin the benefit."

"And I guess they don't mind hurting Randy or us while they're at it," Zoe added darkly. "But who could it be?"

"Allison and Vic?" Bess asked. "They've both been acting suspicious, *and* they were both on the Promenade this afternoon."

"True, but I can't imagine those two working together," George said. "They can't stand each other."

Nancy tapped a forefinger against her chin. "Maybe one of them is working with Tim," she said. "I know that both Vic and Allison have been volunteering for the Heights Gardens benefit, but maybe Tim bribed one of them into helping him sabotage the benefit and make sure Randy couldn't play."

"Maybe, but these are all just guesses," Zoe said, letting out a sigh. "We still don't have any proof as to who abducted Randy and wrecked the Jungle Carousel animals. We might as well head back to the Picnic House. We should at least find something cold to put on that bump, Nancy."

As Zoe turned back toward the path, her flashlight beam flickered over something red in the bushes next to them.

"What's that?" Nancy asked, excited. "Zoe, can you shine that light back here again?"

When Zoe did, Nancy reached out to grab a bit of red yarn caught on a branch. "Hmm," she said, twisting it in her fingers. "This must have torn from my attacker's sweater. Did you guys notice anyone wearing a red sweater back at the Picnic House?"

Zoe, Bess, and George shook their heads. "I wasn't exactly taking a fashion survey," George said. Then she grinned at Nancy. "But you can be sure I will as soon as we get back to the Picnic House."

By the time they reached the building, the pain in Nancy's head had subsided to a dull ache. She saw that the Raving Lunatics were still playing. Allison was right up front, playing guitar and singing a song Nancy didn't recognize.

"She's not wearing a red sweater," Nancy said, as she, Zoe, Bess, and George settled into some folding chairs. She scanned the room. No one else was wearing a red sweater, either.

"There's no way Allison could have been at the carousel if she was practicing with the band," Bess said. "Looks like we've struck out."

"Maybe not," George said in an excited whisper. She nodded toward Allison, raising an eyebrow. "I don't remember that scratch being on her cheek before, do you?"

"You're right!" Nancy said. "And look at her face. It's flushed."

"As if she's been out in the cold?" Zoe asked.

"Or running away from us through the woods," Nancy said, nodding. "Let's find out if the band took a break. If they did, she could have gone to the carousel. We can talk to Peter, Nina, and Julio after the Lunatics stop playing." She put her hand to her head and winced.

"In the meantime, you need some ice for that bump," Zoe said. "There's a store about a block from the park entrance. They'll have ice." She turned to Bess and George. "Any volunteers to come with me?"

"I'll go," Bess said.

Zoe and Bess returned twenty minutes later with some ice wrapped in a towel, and before long the throbbing in Nancy's head had subsided. Just before eleven-thirty, the band broke up for the evening. While Allison unplugged her guitar and put it in the case, Nancy, Zoe, George, and Bess went over to Peter.

"How's everything going?" Zoe asked. "Will you be ready for Friday's concert?"

Peter shot Allison an annoyed look before he answered. "Allison is trying to help us out, but there's no way she'll ever be as good as Randy," he said, keeping his voice low. "Still, it would help if she didn't take off right in the middle of practice."

"She left the building?" Bess asked, shooting Nancy a meaningful glance.

"Yeah," Peter answered. "We agreed on a five-minute break. I figured she just went out for some fresh air. I didn't know she planned on staying out there over half an hour."

Plenty of time to go to the carousel and back, Nancy thought. Turning to Zoe, Bess, and George, she said aloud, "Maybe we should find out for ourselves what she was up to."

"Suit yourselves," Peter told them with a shrug. "You'd better hurry, though. It looks like she's on her way out."

Turning around, Nancy saw that Allison had her jacket on. She was carrying her guitar case and amplifier toward the door. Nancy, Zoe, Bess, and George hurried up to her.

"We can help you with that," Zoe said. She reached for the amplifier, but Allison kept a tight grip on it.

"That's okay, it's just a few more feet." Allison kept her eyes focused on the door up ahead. She didn't seem eager to talk to them.

"Peter says that you went out for some fresh air before," Nancy pressed. "You didn't happen to go to the carousel, did you?"

"T-the carousel?" Allison still wouldn't look at Nancy. She blew a tuft of blond hair off her forehead and picked up her pace. "I don't know what you're talking about."

"No?" Zoe asked. "Well, someone was there, and whoever it was—"

*Honk! Honk!* A car horn sounded from out front.

"There's my dad," Allison said. " 'Bye." She pushed through the Picnic House door, carrying her guitar and amplifier. She stowed the gear in a van parked out front. As Allison got into the van, she shot a panicked glance over her shoulder at Nancy and Zoe.

Nancy was thinking how strong Allison was. Maybe she could have smashed the iron carousel animals after all. The van drove off, and Nancy watched the red taillights fade away.

"We definitely hit a nerve," she said. "Something tells me she knows more about what happened at the carousel than she's letting on."

Zoe nodded, frowning through the glass next to the door. "But once again, Allison weaseled out of giving us a straight answer. Every time we try to talk to her about Randy or the smashed carousel animals, she finds a way to make a quick exit."

"Mmm," said Nancy. "We'll have to find a way to talk to her again—soon. And this time, we have to make sure we get some answers."

"Croissants and cappuccino . . . my favorites," Bess said the following morning. She broke off a piece of the buttery pastry and dunked it in her coffee, then popped it into her mouth. "I think I'm in heaven!"

She, Nancy, George, and Zoe had gotten up early and were having breakfast at a cafe on Montague Street. "This is delicious," Nancy said, taking a bite of her cranberry-ginger muffin. "Just what I need before we go to Allison's."

After talking it over the night before, they'd decided the best place to try to talk to Allison would be at her own house. It wouldn't be easy for Allison to run away from them there.

"It's just after eight," Zoe said, checking her watch. "She's probably still at home, but we don't want to miss her."

George finished her blueberry scone and drank the last sip of her milk. "Say no more. I'm ready to roll," she said.

Within minutes, the four of them were outside. "Allison lives in Cobble Hill," Zoe said, heading south. After walking a few blocks, they stopped at Atlantic Avenue, a busy commercial street, to wait for the light to change. The sun was just rising over the tops of the low buildings, and it slanted right into Nancy's eyes. As she lifted a hand to shade her eyes, she found herself staring at a large sign across the street.

"RiteWay Self-Storage," she read aloud.

"Isn't that where the Brooklyn Players moved all the stuff from their theater?" Bess asked.

Nancy nodded. "We haven't had time to check it out, but as long as we're here"—she raised an eyebrow at the others—"shouldn't we try to get a look in their storage space?"

"Definitely," George said. "If it's a self-service place—where customers do all their own moving and storing—then it's possible Tim is holding Randy captive in their storage space."

"What about Allison?" Zoe asked. "What if she leaves her house? Besides, I have to be at the Anchorage by nine. I'm meeting some other Bradley students to put up the banner for the benefit concert and auction."

"We'll be fast," George promised. "If Randy is there, I don't think we can afford *not* to go."

"Well, when you put it that way." Zoe squared her shoulders, then started across the street as the light changed.

They went into RiteWay Storage and found themselves in a small reception area. A saleswoman stood behind a high counter with brochures on it. A door in back of the counter was propped open. Through the doorway Nancy saw a cavernous space filled with lockers and rolling carts.

"Can I help you?" the woman asked.

"We're with the Brooklyn Players," Nancy said. "We need to get into our storage room, but Tim Chang forgot to tell us which one it is."

Nancy held her breath. A lot of people worked with the theater. She hoped the saleswoman wouldn't question her.

The woman rolled her eyes. "Number 2314," she said. "I wish you people would get organized. You're the sixth person to ask me in the past three days. And I hope you have the key. I'm not authorized to give out our copy."

Nancy, Zoe, George, and Bess were already halfway through the door leading to the storage lockers. "Don't worry, we've got everything we need," Nancy called back. "Thanks!"

As soon as they were out of earshot, Zoe whispered, "But we don't have a key. How are we going to get into the storage room?"

"With this." Nancy reached up and pulled the metal barrette from the end of her french braid.

Room 2314 was halfway down a long aisle whose walls were studded with dozens of doors. A heavy padlock hung from the hasp. Nancy bent close to it and went to work with her barrette.

Zoe pressed her ear against the door and listened for a few moments. "I don't hear anyone moving around . . ."

"If Randy *is* in there, he's probably bound and gagged, so he won't make any noise," George said.

Nancy was too busy working on the lock to

comment. As she twisted the barrette, she felt it connect with the locking mechanism. Carefully, she pushed the barrette a little further in.

"Yes!" she crowed. The padlock clicked open. She slid it from the hasp and opened the storage room door. She, Zoe, Bess, and George leaned in, but the room was pitch-black inside.

"There must be a light switch," George murmured.

As Nancy she felt around inside the door, she heard the *click click* of shoes on the cement floor outside the room.

"Uh-oh," Bess murmured.

Hearing her scared tone, Nancy stepped back out of the storage room—and gasped.

Tim was heading right for them. Angry spots of red colored his cheeks, and his fists were clenched at his side. "I've had it with you bothering me," he said in a deadly serious voice. "This time I'm going to take care of you—once and for all!"

# 12

## Allison's Story

"Wh-what are you talking about?" Bess asked. "There are other people here. You can't—"

"I ought to call the police," Tim said. His angry gaze flicked from Nancy to Bess to Zoe to George.

"Go ahead," Nancy challenged. She faced him and planted her hands on her hips. "Then maybe we'll finally find out exactly what you had to do with sabotaging the Heights Garden benefit auction."

"*And* with Randy La Guardia's disappearance," Zoe added hotly. "We'll be sure to have the police search this storage room when they get here!"

Tim blinked in surprise. "You don't really think . . ." His voice trailed off, and he threw back his head and laughed.

Nancy exchanged confused looks with Zoe,

George, and Bess. Tim wasn't behaving at all as if he was guilty. He was acting as if it were a big joke!

"We heard you say that you wanted the Heights Gardens benefit to flop," George said. "The very next morning someone smashed a valuable carousel animal donated for the auction, *and* Randy was suddenly missing."

"Not to mention that we found one of the Brooklyn Players' masks at the Anchorage, the last place we know Randy was," Bess added. "Do you really expect us to believe you weren't involved?"

The theater director raked an annoyed hand through his straight black hair. "As I told you before, the only thing I'm involved with right now is finding a new theater for the Brooklyn Players," Tim said. He reached inside the storage room, and a moment later a bare lightbulb blinked on overhead. "The only things in here are from the theater. No precious antiques meant for your silly auction. No teenage rock and rollers. If you don't believe me, take a look for yourselves."

The room was jammed with boxes, ladders, stage lights, and costume racks. Nancy didn't see any sign of Randy.

"Now," Tim went on, "will you please leave me alone?"

"What about the mask we found at the Anchorage?" George asked, frowning. "And why did you run away from us when we saw you at Coney Island?"

"I told you the other day, I don't know anything

about the mask," Tim answered. "There were a lot of people at the demonstration. Several masks were lost or burned. I didn't keep track of every single one.

"As for Coney Island, the only reason I was there was to look at a building. I thought the Brooklyn Players might be able to convert it to a theater," he added.

"That run-down old place?" Zoe asked, crinkling up her nose in distaste.

"Once I saw the building, I realized that repairing it was a bigger job than I was willing to take on," Tim said. "It has dozens of safety violations. It wasn't even legal for me to be there. That's why I ducked back inside when I saw you. I never dreamed you'd follow me."

Everything he said made sense, but Nancy still had one more question. "The other day, at the Royale Theater, you really didn't want us up in the tower. Why?" she asked.

"The theater isn't a public place, and I was very busy," Tim said, frowning. "The last thing I needed was for you to fall and hurt yourselves. Besides, you were in the way. We had a lot of boxes stored up in the tower, and I needed to clear them out."

"So, Randy wasn't there?" Bess asked.

The annoyed glimmer came back into Tim's dark eyes. "For the last time, *no*," he answered. "Now, are you going to leave me alone, or am I going to have to call the police?"

Nancy looked closely at Tim. She supposed it was possible he was lying, but her gut feeling was that he was telling the truth. "We're leaving," she told him. "Sorry for all the trouble we've caused you."

"Well, at least we can rule him out as a suspect now," George said, once she, Nancy, Zoe, and Bess were back out on the sidewalk.

"Yes, but the Heights Gardens benefit starts tomorrow," Nancy said. "And we still don't know what happened to Randy *or* who's been sabotaging the auction. I hope we learn something when we talk to Allison."

Zoe frowned, checking her watch. "You three will have to go without me," she said. "I've got to go to the Anchorage to help put up the banner. Good luck!"

"You say Zoe asked you to come talk to me about a special project for the benefit?" Allison asked ten minutes later. Still wearing her bathrobe, she sat down at her family's kitchen table, gesturing for Nancy, Bess, and George to do the same.

Nancy nodded. "Setting up a donation booth for the Heights Gardens at the concert and auction," she said, making up her story as she went along.

Nancy, Bess, and George had arrived as Allison's mother was leaving for work. Allison hadn't seemed happy to find them on her stoop. But at least she'd asked them in. Now that they were here, Nancy was starting to wonder if confronting Allison directly would be a mistake. Allison might get defensive and

110

kick them out. On the other hand, if Nancy could look around a little on the sly, she might find some clue to what, if anything, Allison had to do with Randy's disappearance and the wrecked carousel animals.

"Um, Allison, could I use the bathroom?" Nancy asked. She caught George's eye and nodded subtly toward the staircase they'd seen in the foyer. George gave her a tiny nod to show that she understood.

"Upstairs in the middle of the hall," Allison told her. "I've got to practice with the Raving Lunatics in a while, so if we could hurry—"

"We'll make it quick," Bess cut in. "George and I can fill you in on the project while Nancy's gone."

Tuning out her friends' voices, Nancy went up the stairs to the second floor. She went past the center door, where the bathroom was, and opened the door beyond it. "Bingo," she whispered.

The bedroom she was looking into had to be Allison's. There were posters on the wall and a large collection of rock-and-roll CDs on a shelf next to the bed. A portable phone sat on the desk, along with schoolbooks, makeup, and teen magazines.

I might as well start with the desk, Nancy thought. She hurried over to it and riffled through the books and papers on top. She wasn't even sure what she was looking for, but she didn't find anything unusual.

Next, she opened the top desk drawer. "Pens, erasers, calculator," she murmured. As she reached

111

farther back, her hand hit a crumpled-up wad of paper. She pulled it out, then gently flattened out the creases.

"Whoa," she whispered.

There, in the center of the page, was a note in bold, black capital letters: "DEAD MEN TELL NO TALES. TATTLE TO *ANYONE* ABOUT RANDY, AND YOU'LL BE HISTORY, TOO."

It was the same lettering used on the note Nancy had found among the posters for the benefit! Dozens of questions raced through her mind. Had Allison written the note? Or had she received it from someone else? And what was the secret about Randy that the note writer didn't want revealed? If only . . .

"Allison, wait!" Nancy heard George's frantic voice in the upstairs hall. "Bess and I don't have to see the—"

Before George could finish her sentence, Allison pushed open the door to her room and walked in. Bess and George were right behind her. Allison's mouth dropped open when she saw Nancy. "Hey!" she said angrily. "What are you doing?"

She froze in midstep, her eyes glued to the note in Nancy's hand. The color drained from her face.

"I'd like to know what *you've* been doing lately," Nancy countered. Standing up, she held out the note. "Did you write this?"

"Another note?" Bess asked, looking over Allison's shoulder. "What's going on here?"

"I—uh . . ." Allison shot a panicked glance

around her room. She looked as if she wished she could be anywhere else.

"You could be in big trouble, Allison," George said. "You'd better tell us everything if you don't want to make things worse for yourself."

Allison twisted a strand of blond hair nervously between her fingers. She went over to her bed and sat down with a sigh. "I know you think I did something to hurt Randy," she began, "but I swear I didn't. Whoever wrote that"—she nodded at the note in Nancy's hand—"is the person you're looking for."

"That note makes it sound as if you know what happened to Randy," George said. "And we talked to a Bradley Prep student who said you took off suddenly the night Randy disappeared."

"Look, I admit that I went to the Anchorage that night," Allison said. "But only because I wanted to talk to Randy. I didn't want to hurt him!" She took a deep breath and let it out slowly. "I felt really hurt when the band voted to replace me with Randy. Now that 'Gravity to Go-Go' is on the national charts and the Raving Lunatics might make it big . . . I guess I wanted an apology from Randy for taking away my chance to be a star."

Nancy caught the doubting glances George and Bess exchanged. From everything they had heard, Randy hadn't stolen success from Allison—he'd earned it himself. But Nancy didn't think Allison would appreciate hearing that. "Was Randy in the Anchorage when you got there?" she asked.

"I wasn't sure at first," Allison said, knitting her brows. "I mean, the door was open, and Randy's guitar was still plugged into the amp."

"That's exactly how we found everything Tuesday morning," George murmured.

"But I didn't see Randy anywhere," Allison went on. "I was about to leave when I heard the voices."

"Voices?" Nancy asked, leaning forward.

Allison nodded. "They came from somewhere in the Anchorage. I couldn't tell where—it was so echoey and distorted. I couldn't even tell who was talking or what they were saying." She gave a little shiver and pulled her legs up to sit cross-legged. "All I know is that whoever it was sounded really angry."

"I bet it was Randy and whoever abducted him," George said.

"What about the carousel giraffe?" Bess asked Allison. "Had it been smashed yet?"

Allison gave a helpless shrug. "I don't know. It's not as if I stuck around and made a search," she said. "After I heard those voices, I got really scared. I got out of there as fast as I could."

Nancy stared out Allison's bedroom window, trying to piece together what they'd learned so far. "We found a skeleton mask at the Anchorage. Do you know anything about that?" she asked.

"Oh—I forgot all about the mask," Allison said, snapping her fingers. "I'm the one who left it there. I passed by the Heights Gardens on my way to the Anchorage and saw the Brooklyn Players putting on that demonstration. One of the actors dropped his mask, and I thought it was so cool—"

"You decided to take it," Bess said.

Allison nodded. "I guess I must have dropped it on my way out of the Anchorage," she said. "I didn't think anyone saw me, but the next morning someone slipped an envelope under our front door with my name on it. That note was inside."

"*That's* why you didn't say anything about what you'd seen," Nancy realized. "You were afraid whoever you heard would come after you, too."

"What about last night at the carousel? Someone knocked Nancy out," George said, fixing Allison with a probing look. "You were there, weren't you?"

"Y-yes," Allison said slowly. She bit her lip, looking around her room. "I saw the note about the rendezvous when we were on the Promenade. As soon as I saw the handwriting I knew whoever wrote it was the same person who had threatened me. I guess I wanted to see who it was . . . maybe find out what happened to Randy so that Vic and everyone else would stop looking at *me* like I'm a criminal."

"So when the band took a break," Bess said, "you came to the carousel, too."

"Mmm-hmm," Allison said. "I didn't know what to do when you heard me. I knew if you saw me you'd think I was the one who'd slipped you that note. You guys were getting pretty close to me when that other person ran from behind the carousel and hit you, Nancy. Then the person started running after *me*." Allison shivered, hugging her arms around her knees. "I was lucky to get away."

That fit with what Nancy remembered. Her attacker *had* come from a different direction from the person they'd heard in the brush. "Did you see who the attacker was?" she asked Allison.

Allison shook her head. "Sorry."

"What about Wednesday morning, when the blue carousel tiger was smashed?" George asked. "You were late to practice with the Lunatics, and you didn't give them much of an explanation."

"You think I'd actually ruin anything for the auction? No way!" she said emphatically. "I was just"—her blue eyes flitted briefly from Nancy to Bess to George—"I was making some phone calls, that's all."

Nancy remembered the reporter who'd interviewed the band mentioning an anonymous source. "To the *Brooklyn Heights Bugle*, telling them that you'll be playing with the Lunatics at the benefit concert?"

"Why not?" Allison asked, giving a defiant toss of her head. "If I play at the concert, I deserve to get just as much publicity as Randy." She looked at her watch, then said, "Look, I'm sorry Randy disappeared. I really am. I'd like to help find him, but for now—"

"You have to go practice with the Lunatics," George said.

Nancy didn't miss the sarcastic tone in George's

voice. Allison was pretty selfish, Nancy had to admit. But it was beginning to look as if she wasn't the culprit they were looking for. She, George, and Bess might as well go back to the Anchorage and talk to Zoe about what to do next.

"Come on," Nancy told Allison. "We'll help you with your equipment."

"Hi, Zoe!" Bess called out fifteen minutes later as she, Nancy, and George helped Allison unload her amplifier and guitar from her father's van. "The banner looks great!"

Zoe and a blond young man were on ladders outside the Anchorage entrance. They each held a long red banner between them announcing the Heights Gardens benefit concert and auction in bold colors. Zoe and the man were tying the banner to metal rings set into the massive stone wall of the Anchorage. Half a dozen other students clustered on the ground below, holding the ladders and shouting advice.

"Thanks," Zoe called back.

Nancy caught the curious look Zoe gave Allison. "We'll be right out, Zoe," Nancy said. "Can you take a break so we can talk?"

Zoe gave her the thumbs-up sign. When Nancy, Allison, Bess, and George carried Allison's equipment inside, they found the main room of the Anchorage empty. It took only a moment to deposit the amplifier and guitar on the stage. Nancy was about to go back outside when she heard a noise coming from the room where the auction items were stored. All her senses were instantly on red alert.

"Hello? Is someone there?" she called out.

There was no response.

"Oh, no," George breathed. "You don't think . . ."

Nancy raced down from the stage and hurried into the adjoining room, then let out a sigh of relief. "Oh, it's only you, Mrs. O'Neill," she said.

It looked as if Mrs. O'Neill had just arrived. Her down coat was draped over her forearm, and her canvas tote bag hung from her shoulder. She was standing still and staring at the wall. Upon hearing Nancy, she turned to look at her. Her face was so ashen, it worried Nancy.

"Are you all right, Mrs. O'Neill?" she asked, hurrying over to her.

"Oh, my gosh! It's gone!" Bess cried.

Nancy didn't have to ask what was gone. One look around the room was enough to tell her that the last Jungle Carousel animal was nowhere to be seen.

"The ruby gazelle," Mrs. O'Neill said. "It's gone!"

# 13

## A Desperate Chase

"The gazelle?" George whipped her head from side to side. "Oh, no!"

"I—I arrived a few moments ago," Mrs. O'Neill said slowly, continuing to stare at the space where the gazelle had been. "The ruby . . . the ruby red gazelle was . . . gone." She was so distraught, she could barely get the words out. "I've got to get it back or everything will be ruined!"

Nancy was upset, too, but she knew they had to stay calm if they wanted any chance of finding the gazelle. "Who could have taken it?" she wondered aloud.

"Vic?" Bess asked.

"He sure seems to hate Randy, but that doesn't mean he took the gazelle or wrecked the other two carousel animals," George said.

Nancy thought she saw Mrs. O'Neill blink at the mention of Vic's name. An angry gleam came into her hazel eyes, but she said nothing.

"Someone from the neighborhood watch must have been here during the night," Nancy said, thinking out loud. "Until Zoe got here, anyway."

"And Zoe and the others have been right outside since then," Bess added. "It's not as if someone could come in here and take a huge cast-iron animal without anyone noticing it."

"I'll ask if they saw anything," Allison said, and ran from the room.

Nancy was still lost in thought. "Maybe the person didn't *leave* with the gazelle," she said suddenly. "Maybe he's still right here in the Anchorage!"

"The tunnels . . . Of course!" Mrs. O'Neill said. Her eyes lit up with a fiery determination. Letting her coat fall to the floor, she hurried to the door and grabbed the metal flashlight from the hook. "You girls stay here. I'm going after Vic."

"We can't be sure it's him," Nancy said. "Shouldn't we call the police?"

Mrs. O'Neill shook her head firmly. "There's not enough time."

She started toward the tunnels, but George grabbed her arm. "You have to at least let us go with you. What if the person is armed?"

"I won't have you put yourselves in danger," Mrs. O'Neill said, frowning. "I'm responsible for—"

"Nancy! Mrs. O'Neill!" Zoe cried, racing into the room. "Allison just told us. Is it true? Is the gazelle really . . ." Her voice trailed off as she gazed at the empty spot. "It *is* gone," she said in a horrified whisper. "But I don't see how—I mean, Julio's dad was here all night keeping an eye on things for the neighborhood watch. When he let me in this morning, he said that everything was fine."

"What about the gazelle? Did you see it?" Mrs. O'Neill asked. She clutched the flashlight so tightly that her knuckles were white.

Zoe nodded. "It was here when we picked up the banner and ladders and stuff." She ran a hand distractedly through her dark, wavy hair. "I don't think anyone I'm with could have taken it. No one was alone in here long enough. No one else even showed up here until you did, Mrs. O'Neill. You and—"

Zoe broke off suddenly, and her eyes flew around the room. "Where's Vic?" she asked.

"Vic Wollenski?" Nancy asked, blinking in surprise. "Why? Did *he* come into the Anchorage?"

Zoe let out a groan. "Yes. I can't believe I didn't think of it sooner. He came in about ten minutes before you did, Mrs. O.," she said. "I'm sure I didn't see him come out again."

"Which means that Nancy's right," George said. "He must still be here in the tunnels!"

"That little— He's not getting away with this," Mrs. O'Neill said. Pulling away from George, she took off into the Anchorage's dark tunnels.

Bess stared after Mrs. O'Neill, her eyes wide with worry. "We're not going to let her go by herself, are we?" she asked.

121

"No way," Nancy answered. "Come on!"

She hurried out of the room and stared in the direction Mrs. O'Neill had taken. The dark, shadowy tunnel was lit only by Mrs. O'Neill's flashlight. She was going around a corner a dozen or so yards ahead. Her bright beam disappeared from view, but Nancy could still see a faint glow lighting up the dank walls.

"Mrs. O., wait up!" Zoe called. "We don't have a flashlight."

The glow from Mrs. O'Neill's flashlight grew dimmer up ahead. "We'll have to catch up, that's all. I'm pretty sure I have my penlight," Nancy said. She dug into her shoulder bag, pulling out the pocket-size flashlight. She flicked it on and started into the tunnels. "Everyone stay close."

"You can count on it," Bess said in a shaky voice.

Within moments they rounded the corner Mrs. O'Neill had taken. Nancy spotted her silhouette about thirty feet ahead. Her flashlight beam was splayed out against the dank tunnel in front of her. "Hurry. Maybe we can catch up—"

"Shh!" George hissed, holding a hand up in the semidarkness. "Listen!"

A faint hammering sound of metal on metal was coming from somewhere deep within the tunnels. Nancy couldn't tell exactly where it came from, but she had a feeling she knew what it was. "Vic . . . He must be trying to smash the gazelle!"

"Oh, no. We've got to find him—and fast," Bess said.

As they hurried forward, Mrs. O'Neill disappeared around another corner up ahead. "No wonder she's not waiting for us," Nancy murmured. "Delaying even a second could mean Vic will destroy the gazelle before we get there!"

Scrambling through the darkness, they wound around the next corner and the next. Each time they came to a new tunnel, Mrs. O'Neill's flashlight beam seemed farther and farther ahead. As Nancy followed with George, Bess, and Zoe, her penlight barely lit up the brick walls and rough stone floor. Nancy felt a knot of worry twist tighter in her stomach whenever the banging hammer echoed out.

As they turned into yet another tunnel, Zoe stopped. "Uh-oh, now I don't see Mrs. O. at all," she said.

Nancy stopped and shone her penlight ahead. All she saw were brick walls disappearing into thick blackness. "I can't even tell if we're closer to the hammering," she said, frowning. "The stone walls make it sound as if the noise is coming from everywhere at once."

"Are we lost?" Bess asked, her voice barely a whisper.

"I don't know," Nancy said. Taking a deep breath, she shone her penlight around and tried to get her bearings. Her beam lit up a few wooden crates and a chipped sheet of plywood leaning against the wall right next to them. "Isn't this the same stuff we saw the other day, when we found Vic back in the tunnels . . . ?"

"Beats me," George said. "We've taken so many turns, I feel as if we must be in a different state by now."

"Mmm," Nancy murmured, leaning against the plywood. The crates and plywood looked familiar, but it was hard to think, with the sound of the sledgehammer echoing around her. Sometimes the noise seemed so far away. Then it would sound much closer. "We've got to find a way to . . ."

She let her voice trail off as she heard the noise again. It wasn't the metallic hammering, she realized. It was more muffled, and it seemed to shake the board she was leaning against. "That pounding," she said. "It sounds like it's right next to us."

"It *is* coming from right behind us!" Zoe cried.

Nancy whirled around and grabbed one side of the plywood. "Help me move this thing," she said.

Zoe grabbed the other side, and they slid the board to the side. Nancy ran her penlight beam over the area the board had covered, and she gasped. "Hey! This is a door!"

*Thump! Thump!*

The noise sounded from the other side of the wooden door, followed by a muffled cry. This time Nancy was positive it wasn't her imagination or her ears playing tricks on her.

Turning to her friends, she said, "Someone's in there!"

# 14

## Lost—and Found

"Oh, my gosh!" Zoe exclaimed. She bent close to the door and called, "Randy, is that you?"

The pounding from the other side of the door grew more intense.

"It *must* be him!" said Bess.

Nancy tugged on the door handle, but the door didn't budge. Two boards were nailed across the door and into the wooden frame. "We've got to find a way to pry these boards off," she said.

She shone her penlight over the ground, looking for something she could use. She'd only covered a small area when she heard George mutter, "Ouch!" Then came the metallic clatter of something skidding across the floor.

"Hey," George cried. She bent down and picked up a hammer.

"Whoever locked up Randy must have kept it hidden behind the plywood," Nancy said, "so he could take the boards off and put them on when he came to see Randy."

"Vic," Zoe said. "He did this, I know it. He wasn't just exploring when we found him back here. He was doing something to Randy!"

She grabbed the hammer from George and eagerly went to work on the boards. "These things are really nailed in tight," she said. She gritted her teeth, yanking at the boards with the clawed end of the hammer. "But don't worry, Randy. We'll get you out of there soon."

Another metallic clank echoed in the tunnels. It was followed seconds later by angry voices.

"Uh-oh," said Bess. "Sounds like Mrs. O'Neill found Vic."

"She could be in trouble," Nancy said. She peered into the tunnel Mrs. O'Neill had taken. "I'm going after them."

"Me, too," George said.

"I'd better stick around here," Bess said, shooting a worried look at the wooden door. "I hope Randy's not hurt. But if he is . . ."

"He may need some kind of help," Zoe said, without stopping her work. Glancing over her shoulder at Nancy and George, she added, "We'll call the police and find you guys after we get Randy out."

Nancy hesitated, shining her penlight on the

door. "Are you sure you'll be all right without any light?" she asked.

"We'll manage," Zoe said. "Don't worry."

Nancy's heart pounded as she and George hurried down the dark tunnel. Her penlight illuminated the shadowy, uneven walls and the tense look on George's face beside her. After about twenty yards, they stopped next to a dark opening in the wall to their right.

"This way?" George asked.

Nancy cocked her head to one side and listened, then nodded. "The voices are definitely coming from down there. And look! I see light."

A dozen yards ahead, a towering pile of old wooden crates was lit up from behind by the glow from a flashlight. Nancy could hear Mrs. O'Neill talking to someone who sounded like Vic. Their voices were angry, and their distorted black shadows made flickering, ghoulish shapes on the walls.

"I hope Vic's not trying to hurt her," George said grimly.

"Mrs. O'Neill!" Nancy called out, picking up her pace. "It's Nancy and George. We're coming!"

As they raced around the pile of crates, Nancy saw the gazelle. It was lying on its side between the crates and the walls at the end of the tunnel. A flashlight on the ground lit up the gazelle—and Vic, who was standing over it. He wore a red wool sweater over his shirt and jeans. In his hands was a sledgehammer. Mrs. O'Neill stood a few feet away, holding the flashlight she'd taken from the auction room. She and Vic stopped talking when they saw Nancy and George.

"Put the hammer down, Vic," Nancy ordered, slipping her penlight into her back pocket.

When he hesitated, George said, "We know you hid Randy in a room back here in the tunnels. As soon as Zoe and Bess get him out, he's going to tell the police the whole story."

"What!" Mrs. O'Neill cried. Her anxious gaze flew to the gazelle. Then she seemed to catch herself. "That's just what I've been trying to get him to do," she said to Nancy and George. "But we've got to hurry!"

What's going on here? Nancy wondered. Why did Mrs. O'Neill seem worried about the police?

"*You're* going to try to lock *me* up?" Vic said bitterly. "That's a laugh."

"You'll pay for what you've done, you little thief," Mrs. O'Neill said in a deadly serious voice. She took a step toward Vic, and he raised the sledgehammer.

"No!" Nancy gasped. She lunged forward and grabbed the sledgehammer before Vic could swing it. He tried to pull it from her grasp, but George grabbed his arms from behind. Vic was forced to let go of the sledgehammer. Nancy pushed it safely out of reach. Within seconds, she and George were holding Vic's arms behind his back.

"Good work," Mrs. O'Neill said. An intense determined glow filled her eyes. "Let's tie him up.

Then I'll return the gazelle and call the police while you wait with Vic."

"Don't listen to her!" Vic cried out, struggling against Nancy and George. *"She's* the one who should go to—"

Mrs. O'Neill clamped a hand over his mouth. "That's enough," she said. She dropped her flashlight and began rooting through her canvas bag with her free hand. "I know I've got twine in here and something to use as a gag."

Nancy wasn't about to let go of Vic, but she couldn't help wondering about Mrs. O'Neill, too. Why was she so determined to keep Vic from talking? And why did she still seem so agitated? After all, now that Vic had been subdued, the gazelle was safe. Judging by the concerned way George was looking at Mrs. O'Neill, she was wondering the same thing.

"Mrs. O'Neill?" Nancy began. "The police will be here soon. We don't have to—"

"Aha!" Mrs. O'Neill said triumphantly. She held up a ball of twine and a handkerchief, letting her canvas bag slide to the ground. The first thing she did was press the handkerchief over Vic's mouth. "Help me tie him up," she told Nancy and George.

Mrs. O'Neill was already unwinding twine, but Nancy hesitated. She couldn't stifle the feeling that something was wrong. But everything was happening so fast, she couldn't put her finger on what it was.

As Mrs. O'Neill began to wrap twine over the

handkerchief, the toe of her sneaker caught on her canvas bag. The bag tipped over, sending an avalanche of keys, papers, change purse, and other things onto the uneven floor. A framed, yellowed newspaper photograph slid out on top of the pile. It caught Nancy's attention immediately.

"The Jungle Carousel," she whispered.

Mrs. O'Neill was so busy tying up Vic that she didn't seem to have heard. Nancy bent over the photo to get a better look. It was the famous Jungle Carousel all right. Nancy spotted the giraffe, tiger, and gazelle, along with an elephant, a zebra, and dozens of other animals circling the carousel.

This must be the photograph Sammy Altman donated for the auction! Nancy's mind screamed out.

She wasn't sure why she didn't say anything aloud. A sixth sense warned her to keep quiet. When Nancy had asked about the photograph, Mrs. O'Neill had said she didn't remember seeing it. Obviously, she'd been lying. But why?

Nancy shot Mrs. O'Neill a quick look, but she was still bent over Vic. She was working the twine around his wrists now. Putting a finger to her lips, Nancy gestured for George to look at the photograph, too.

Three people were pictured standing in front of the carousel: an older man, a younger man, and a little girl, who was holding a doll. The caption below the photograph read: "Famous Cat Burglar Nabbed at Coney Island."

130

Nancy felt her heart start to beat faster. She had a feeling she knew exactly who the cat burglar was. As she read on, her hunch was confirmed: "Anthony Patrick Kennedy, also known as the Glove, was apprehended yesterday at Coney Island. . . ."

Nancy exchanged a look with George. So there *was* a connection between the Glove and the Jungle Carousel!

She read the rest of the caption: "The Glove is pictured here in a family photo taken at the Seafoam Palace amusement park the day before his arrest. With him are his father, Anthony Kennedy, Sr., and his five-year-old daughter, Margaret Kennedy. The doll held by Margaret is one of the items the Glove stole from a Brooklyn Heights brownstone during his latest theft. The doll—and the ruby ring hidden inside—have yet to be recovered."

Nancy blinked in surprise as she read the final sentence. So, she thought, the Glove's daughter may have been the last one to have the ruby ring!

Nancy's eyes kept jumping back to the girl's name. Margaret Kennedy. She'd heard that name before, she was sure of it. Nancy lightly tapped the glass over the picture, trying to remember.

"That's it!" she said.

Mrs. O'Neill jerked her head around. When she saw Nancy and George bent over the photograph, her eyes widened in surprise. "What are you doing with that?" she demanded. All the warmth was gone from her round face, replaced by a cold look of displeasure.

"Yesterday," Nancy said slowly, "when we met Mr. O'Neill at that cafe, he called you *Margaret Kennedy* O'Neill," she began. She could hardly believe what she was thinking. But as she mulled the whole thing over, she became more and more certain she was right.

"You're the little girl in the picture, Mrs. O'Neill," Nancy went on. She held up the photograph, pointing at the caption. "You're the Glove's daughter! And I think you know exactly what happened to the ruby ring."

# 15

## The Secret of the Ruby Gazelle

"Wow!" George breathed. She gaped at Mrs. O'Neill as if she were looking at a character who'd popped out of an old movie.

Mrs. O'Neill frowned and gave a final tug to the twine around Vic's wrists. "That's utter nonsense," she sputtered. "Maybe the Glove was my father, but I was only a little girl when that ruby ring was stolen. How could I possibly know what he did with it?"

"You *are* holding the doll in this picture," George pointed out. "That happens to be exactly where the ring was hidden."

Nancy noticed the way Mrs. O'Neill's eyes flitted nervously toward the gazelle. More and more pieces of the mystery were falling into place. "Your family's Jungle Carousel burned down two days after the Glove was arrested. And now someone is suddenly breaking open animals from the same carousel," Nancy said. "What if someone—either you or your father or grandfather—hid the ruby ring inside one of the carousel animals?"

One look at Mrs. O'Neill's face and Nancy knew she'd guessed correctly.

"That would explain a lot," George said. "Such as why someone has been breaking *only* the carousel animals and nothing else. We thought someone was trying to sabotage the auction, but—"

"But it was *you*, Mrs. O'Neill," Nancy said. "You were trying to get the ruby ring back, weren't you?"

Vic had been twisting and squirming against the twine while they spoke. All at once, he spat the handkerchief free of his mouth. "She *was* after the ring . . . and she got me to help her," he said. He glared at Mrs. O'Neill before going on. "Of course, she was only going to pay me a thousand dollars. She didn't mention that the ring was priceless."

Nancy recalled that Vic had been interested in hearing about the Glove and the ruby ring on the Promenade the day before. Now she knew why. He was scheming to help Mrs. O'Neill steal it! Nancy still wasn't sure why the two hated each other so much now, but she had more important things to find out first.

"So you two came here Monday night," she said. "What you didn't realize was that Randy would show up, too. He saw what you two were doing, didn't he?"

"He showed up right after we'd broken the

giraffe," Mrs. O'Neill said, frowning. "Luckily, Vic and I were able to overpower him and hide him in one of the rooms back here. I checked out these tunnels carefully when we were considering where to hold the benefit concert and auction, so I knew the room was there."

George turned to Vic, shaking her head in disgust. "You weren't exploring back here the other day, were you?" she said. "You must have come back here to check on Randy."

"Not that it did me any good," Vic grumbled. "I brought him some food, but as soon as I took off his gag, he started yelling. I barely had time to tie him up and lock him in again before you found me."

"That's why you pretended to have sprained your ankle, so we'd think that *you'd* called out, not Randy," Nancy said.

"After we got Randy out of the way, we planned to go to work on the tiger and this gazelle," Mrs. O'Neill continued. "But then we were interrupted again—"

"By Allison," George said. "She already told us she was here that night. We saw the threatening note you left her, to make sure she wouldn't say anything."

"You left that note about the rendezvous at the Prospect Park Carousel, too," Nancy added, turning to Vic. "You must have put it in the bag while you were getting more posters."

Vic nodded, his blue eyes flashing angrily. "At least Allison had enough sense to obey the note.

But *you* wouldn't stop trying to find out what had happened to Randy and the carousel animals— even after I gave you that warning," he said.

"That attack was more than just a warning," George said, planting her hands on her hips. "You could have killed Nancy!"

Vic shrugged. It made Nancy shiver to see how callous he was acting. "We had to get the ring," he said. "Once the neighborhood watch started, it was practically impossible to smash the animals without being seen. Mrs. O'Neill was lucky no one else was around when she got here on Wednesday morning."

"I didn't think I'd be able to break the blue tiger open by myself," Mrs. O'Neill said, "but I had to try."

"I guess you succeeded, because when Peter, Nina, and Julio got here, the blue tiger had already been smashed to bits," Nancy said.

Mrs. O'Neill gave a nod. "The rust spots on the tiger had weakened the metal just enough to enable me to shatter it. Everything worked out perfectly, except that the ruby ring wasn't inside." She shook her head sadly, then glared at Vic. "If I'd known I could break open the animals on my own, I never would have asked *him* to help me."

"You tried to cheat me!" Vic cried, but Mrs. O'Neill ignored him.

"I shouldn't have trusted him," she said, giving a bitter shake of her head. "Yesterday he called my house and demanded a hundred thousand dollars. I refused, of course."

Nancy looked back and forth from Vic to Mrs. O'Neill. They were both acting outraged. It didn't seem to occur to them that they were breaking the law. Nancy couldn't believe how twisted their priorities had become.

"So Vic got here ahead of you today and tried to get the ruby ring for himself," George said.

"He tried. But he won't succeed. No one's going to stop me from getting that ruby," Mrs. O'Neill said, in a deadly serious voice.

In the next instant she lunged for the sledgehammer, which was lying next to the gazelle. Before Nancy could get to her, Mrs. O'Neill grabbed the hammer and swung it in a threatening arc.

"Whoa!" Nancy had to jump back to keep the head from slamming into her stomach. She, George, and Vic were cornered at the end of the tunnel. Mrs. O'Neill blocked the only way out, past the pile of wooden crates and back through the tunnels.

"You two do exactly as I say, or you'll never get out of this tunnel alive," Mrs. O'Neill said. She gestured toward Vic with her head. "Get over there," she ordered. "George, you tie Nancy's wrists."

Nancy caught the helpless look on George's face. All she could do was shrug in response. That sledgehammer looked as if it could do a lot of damage. They couldn't overpower Mrs. O'Neill without taking the risk of getting seriously injured.

After Nancy's wrists were bound with twine, Mrs. O'Neill tied George's wrists together, too. Within minutes, Nancy, George, and Vic were sitting against the wall. Mrs. O'Neill went to work on the ruby gazelle, pounding it with the sledgehammer. Nancy cringed when she saw the hammer crash down on the rusted patches on the gazelle's legs and haunches.

She looked past the crates but didn't see or hear the others coming. What was taking them so long? She had to do something—anything—to stall for time.

"What exactly happened back in 1941?" she asked Mrs. O'Neill. "How did the ruby end up inside one of the carousel animals?"

Mrs. O'Neill stopped hammering for a moment. A faraway look came into her eyes. "I didn't know my father was . . . well, that he took things from people."

"You mean, that he *stole* things," George said dryly. "He was a thief, Mrs. O'Neill."

"He was desperate!" Mrs. O'Neill insisted, leaning on the sledgehammer's handle. "It was the Depression. Times were hard, and we didn't have much. All my father did was take a few things from people who already had more than enough. I don't see what's so terrible about that."

Nancy stared at Mrs. O'Neill in disbelief. "Stealing a ruby ring worth hundreds of thousands of dollars is a serious crime," she said.

"He didn't even know he had the ring," Mrs. O'Neill said. "The only reason he took the doll was because he wanted to give me something new to play with." With that, she lifted the sledgehammer and began pounding the gazelle again.

"Why didn't the police find the doll when they recovered the rest of the stolen things?" George asked. "What did you do with it?"

"I used to play near the Jungle Carousel when my grandfather and father worked," Mrs. O'Neill said breathlessly. "After my father gave me the doll, I took it there. My father was arrested at our apartment. That's where he'd hidden the rest of the things he'd taken, under floorboards in the kitchen. I guess it took the police a day to realize that the doll was still missing . . ."

"And the ruby ring," Nancy pointed out.

"Yes," said Mrs. O'Neill. "It wasn't until the police came to the carousel, looking for the doll, that I realized *I* had the ruby. I was terrified! I thought they were going to arrest me, too."

Mrs. O'Neill's face was red and sweaty from swinging the sledgehammer. She wiped her brow with the back of her arm, then kept hammering. "While the police were talking to my grandfather, I ran and found the doll in the workshop, where we did repairs," she explained. "It was right next to the Jungle Carousel, and that was where I'd left the doll. I twisted off its head, and sure enough, there it was—a gold ring with the biggest, reddest jewel you could imagine."

She shook her head, as if she still couldn't believe it. "I didn't know what to do, so I just shoved it inside one of the carousel animals that my grandfather was repairing. He'd removed the leather tail to replace it, and the hole was just big enough . . ."

Mrs. O'Neill stopped hammering to catch her breath. "Of course, I had no idea the carousel would burn to the ground just days later," she went on, "along with the rest of the Seafoam Palace. I was sure the ruby was gone forever."

"Until Sam Altman wheeled the jungle animals in here the other day," George said.

Thinking back, Nancy remembered that Mrs. O'Neill had reacted strongly to the animals. At the time, she'd thought it was just because they were so unusual. Now she knew the real reason.

Nancy looked past the wooden crates once more, then sighed. There were no signs of Zoe, Bess, or Randy. "It's an amazing story," she said. "But I still don't understand something. Why break all three carousel animals? Why not just go straight for the one that has the ruby?"

"So much time had passed. I couldn't remember which one it was," Mrs. O'Neill said. She frowned, brushing a lock of gray hair from her face. "And I couldn't simply buy the animals at the auction. Money's been tight since my husband was laid off. I wasn't sure I'd be able to outbid everyone else. I knew if I wanted that ruby, I was just going to have to take it."

She raised the hammer once again over her head

and brought it down on the cast-iron gazelle with a tremendous bang. The gazelle's entire rusted haunch crumbled. All Nancy could do was watch in horror. Mrs. O'Neill brought the sledgehammer down one, two, three more times. Within seconds, the rest of the gazelle had broken to pieces.

Dropping the sledgehammer, Mrs. O'Neill kneeled down and began frantically digging through the cast-iron bits that had formed the gazelle's hooves. "If it's in here, it would have dropped to the bottom," she murmured.

She gasped and plucked something from the ground.

"Wow," George said, her mouth falling open.

Nancy could hardly believe her eyes. A glimmer of light from the flashlight reflected off a sparkling, deep red ruby. Nancy had never before seen a gem so large.

"Finally . . . after all these years," Mrs. O'Neill murmured. She stared greedily at the ruby, then clutched it tightly in her fist. "It's mine."

"Nancy! George!" Zoe's voice came from the tunnels.

"Oh, no!" Mrs. O'Neill gasped. She turned around as Zoe and Bess ran past the towering pile of crates. Randy was with them. His face and clothes were smudged with dirt, but he didn't seem to be injured. He glared at Mrs. O'Neill while Zoe and Bess rushed over to Nancy, George, and Vic.

"Randy just told us *you're* the one who locked

him up," Zoe said, turning to Mrs. O'Neill. There was a betrayed look on her face, as if she couldn't quite believe it. "How could you?"

Mrs. O'Neill's gaze flitted nervously over all the eyes staring at her. She looked like a deer caught in the beam of a car's headlights. "You don't understand. The ruby ring is mine," she said slowly. "Getting it back means my husband and I will never have to worry about money again."

She bolted and raced past Randy. As she rounded the pile of crates, she tugged at them, sending them crashing across the tunnel.

"We're blocked in!" Randy cried in dismay. "She's going to get away!"

"What about the police? Did you call them?" George asked Zoe and Bess.

Zoe shook her head. "Once Randy told us about Mrs. O'Neill, we ran back here first thing," she said.

"Quick! Untie us," Nancy said. "If we can dig out fast enough, we can still catch up with her."

Within moments Nancy, George, and Vic were free. They hurried to help Randy, who was already pulling crates away from the pile. Nancy reached for the nearest crate, then stopped and sniffed the air.

"That's smoke," she realized.

Hot wisps of it filtered through the wooden crates, clogging the air. Seconds later Nancy heard the crackling of flames.

"Mrs. O'Neill set the crates on fire!" Bess said in a horrified whisper. "We're trapped!"

# 16

## Terror in the Anchorage

Nancy watched in horror as flames danced into the air near one wall. Within seconds they were spreading across the blockade of wooden crates. Already the hot, acrid smoke stung her lungs, making her cough.

"The fire's moving fast," she said urgently. "We don't have long before . . ."

The rest of her words were lost in a fit of coughing. The smoke was getting thicker. She could feel it choking off the air in the tunnel. Randy, Zoe, Bess, George, and Vic were all coughing, too, their faces red and sweaty.

"Hurry!" Vic said.

None of them had to be told twice. They leaped at the part of the pile that wasn't yet in flames, frantically pulling crates out of the way. But every time they cleared some away, more fell from the top of the pile to block the way.

"Look out!" Zoe cried. She pulled Randy back just in time to save him from being hit by a flaming crate that toppled from above.

Randy jumped back, then quickly kicked the crate into a corner, where it couldn't ignite anything else. "Thanks, Zoe," he said, shivering. "You saved me . . . again."

"We're not . . . out of trouble . . . yet," Zoe said. She was coughing so much, she could hardly speak. As she pulled at more crates, she tried to wave away the blanket of smoke that settled ever more thickly around them.

"Cover your nose and mouth!" Nancy said, quickly pulling up the neck of her own T-shirt until the fabric covered the lower half of her face. "And stay low to the ground, where the smoke and heat aren't as bad."

"It's useless!" Bess moaned, wiping her brow with the back of her hand. "Look!"

The flames were almost completely across the pile of crates now, Nancy saw. "If we want to get out of here, we've got to do it now!" she cried. Keeping as low as she could, she jumped toward the crates and grabbed one that wasn't on fire yet. "Quick—everyone take a crate. We'll have to try to push our way through. We can use these as shields."

George stared grimly at the growing wall of fire. "But, what if . . ."

"It's our only hope," Vic cut in. He grabbed a crate, tossing others to Randy, Zoe, Bess, and George. "Stay close to this side," he said, waving to the crates that weren't yet on fire. "We can push through in a line."

Nancy nodded and held up her crate. Everyone else looked as worried as she felt, but they lined up with their crates in front of them. "Okay," Nancy said. "One . . . two . . . three . . . Go!"

They charged forward. A second later Nancy felt her crate hit the pile, and she pushed into it with every ounce of strength she could muster. "Yes!" she cried as she felt crates give way.

Crates and smoke and flames were all around her. The air was so hot that Nancy felt she surely must be on fire. She squeezed her eyes shut and pushed blindly forward.

"We did it!" Bess's amazed voice came from right next to Nancy.

Nancy opened her eyes, her breath heaving inside her chest. They were on the *other* side of the crates now, she saw. She stumbled away from the flames, feeling weak with relief. The fire was behind them.

"Not a moment too soon," George said. She stared grimly at the inferno, which had now spread across the entire width of the tunnel.

"We've got to get out of here and call the fire

department—and the police," Zoe said. She let her crate clatter to the ground and stared into the dark tunnel ahead. "Mrs. O'Neill could be getting away!"

"Follow me," Vic said, pressing his mouth into a determined line. "I know the way."

"Why should we trust *you?*" Randy asked, glancing dubiously at Vic. "You're the one who locked me up in the first place, remember?"

Vic glared into the dark tunnels, his sweater still pulled over his nose and mouth. "Mrs. O'Neill was going to let us *die* in that fire," he said. "I'm not going to let her get away with that."

"Vic *did* help us to escape from the fire," Nancy said. "Besides, what other choice do we have?"

As Vic scrambled forward into the tunnels, she, Randy, Zoe, Bess, and George hurried after him. A few minutes later, Nancy saw the main room of the Anchorage come into sight up ahead. They'd done it!

As soon as they reached the huge, open room, Bess ran outside for the phone. "I'll call the police and fire department!" she cried.

"Have them send a patrol car to Mrs. O'Neill's house," Vic said. "Sixty-four Willow Street!"

Vic dashed for the entrance, with Nancy, Randy, George, and Zoe behind him. Just before he reached the door, Allison pulled it open from the outside. "What happened?" she asked, looking at their sweaty, stained faces. "Why do you guys smell like a campfire? Randy!" she cried when she saw him. "You're all right!"

"No time to explain," he said curtly. "Just stay out of the Anchorage!" He raced past Allison, heading outside.

Nancy barely noticed the curious faces of the students outside. She, Randy, Zoe, and George were right behind Vic as he took the lead. They ran up the hill to the street that ran parallel to the Promenade. Just after they got to the Heights Gardens, Vic swung left onto Orange Street.

"I've been to Mrs. O.'s before, too," Zoe said breathlessly. "Willow Street is the next street we come to. She lives right at the corner."

"There she is!" Randy cried, pointing.

Glancing ahead to the end of the block, Nancy spotted Mrs. O'Neill. She was pulling a suitcase down the steps of a two-story brick house. Mr. O'Neill was on the sidewalk in front, loading another bag into a parked car.

"Stop!" George cried.

Mrs. O'Neill's mouth dropped open in horror. "Oh, no! How did . . . ?"

She didn't finish her question. Letting her suitcase drop to the sidewalk, she took off the other way down the street.

"You're not getting away this time," Nancy heard Vic mutter under his breath.

Half a dozen pounding strides later, he and Nancy caught up with Mrs. O'Neill. Nancy grabbed her coat sleeve, while Vic dived for her arms. Moments later they were holding her arms twisted behind her back.

"Let . . . me . . . go!" she said between clenched teeth.

"Not a chance," Nancy said. Looking over her shoulder, she saw George, Randy, and Zoe holding Mr. O'Neill next to the car. "You might as well give up, Mrs. O'Neill. It's over."

"The Raving Lunatics sound great!" Bess said Friday evening.

"That's for sure. Ever since they started playing, I haven't been able to keep still," Nancy said. She grinned at Bess, George, and Zoe, nodding her head to the music.

The four of them had front-row seats at the Heights Gardens benefit concert. The fire department had put out the fire, and volunteers had cleaned up the debris. A bitter smoky scent still hung on the air, but it hadn't kept anyone from the concert. Looking around, Nancy saw that every seat in the Anchorage was filled. There were even people standing in the aisles and behind the chairs. As Randy finished a short guitar solo, they erupted in wild applause and cheers.

"Being locked up for three days sure didn't hurt Randy's performance," George said. "Look at this crowd. They love him!"

Zoe nodded, her dark eyes gleaming. "He sounds

better than ever," she agreed. "Thanks to him and the rest of the band, we've already raised over thirty thousand dollars for the Heights Gardens renovation. We could bring in even more than that at tomorrow's auction . . . no thanks to Mrs. O'Neill."

Zoe let out a deep sigh and shook her head. "I still can't believe it. I mean, Mrs. O'Neill worked so hard for the Heights Gardens benefit. How could she wreck those beautiful Jungle Carousel animals? *And* leave us in that fire? It's as if nothing meant a thing to her anymore except the ruby ring."

Nancy's heart went out to Zoe. It had to hurt to find out that someone she trusted was capable of being so destructive. "Greed and desperation can make people do awful things," she said. "What's important is that Mrs. O'Neill is in jail now."

"And that Vic will be doing community service to pay for what he did," George added.

Vic had told the police the part he'd played in destroying the carousel giraffe and locking up Randy in the Anchorage. Since Vic had helped free everyone from the fire and capture Mrs. O'Neill, Randy and his parents had agreed not to press for a more serious punishment.

"I wonder what's going to happen to the ruby ring now?" Bess asked. "Zoe, didn't you say the police were tracking down the family it originally belonged to?"

"Oh! I forgot to tell you," Zoe said. "The police

149

called this morning to say they talked to the family. After hearing the whole story, the family decided to donate the ring for the Heights Garden auction!"

"Wow," Nancy said. "Now you'll definitely have enough money to renovate the park."

"And to set up a fund to maintain it in the future," Zoe said. "Isn't that great?"

Nancy had to agree that it was. She was just turning her attention back to the stage when the band came to the end of a song and Randy announced that they were taking a break.

"Don't go away," his amplified voice boomed from the speakers. "We'll be back in a few minutes."

"Let's go talk to the band," Zoe said, getting to her feet.

As they merged with the stream of people moving into the aisles, Nancy caught sight of Allison's short blond hair ahead of them. "Allison!" she called, waving. "How do you like the concert?"

Allison gave an offhand shrug. "It's all right, I guess," she said.

Nancy exchanged wry looks with George, Zoe, and Bess. Apparently, Allison still thought that *she* should be the star of the band. "It must be a little disappointing not to play," Bess said, "after all the time you spent practicing with the band."

"No way," Allison said right away. "One thing I've learned over the last few days is that it's stupid to hold a grudge. I'm glad Randy's all right, and I'm not going to waste any more time crying over the Lunatics." She gave a smug smile. "I've got better things to do . . . like start my own band. An all-girl band, I think. And when I do, people will be talking about *us*, not the Raving Lunatics."

With that, Allison turned around and kept going. George stared after her, rolling her eyes. "She's too much," she said. "But at least Randy doesn't have to worry about her threatening him anymore."

When Zoe, George, Nancy, and Bess finally made it to the stage, Randy rushed over to give them hugs. "This crowd is great," he said. "They make us feel like real celebrities." His blue eyes were gleaming with pleasure, and he was looking everywhere at once.

"You are," Zoe said, grinning at him. "You guys sound terrific."

"Thanks," Randy said. He gulped some water from a plastic bottle. "We even got a compliment from Tim Chang."

"You're kidding," Nancy said. "I'm surprised he would even come to the concert, considering that he's against the Heights Gardens benefit."

"He came by the Anchorage while we were setting up," Randy explained. "He was with some guy from the city's cultural affairs office. Apparently, now that the Brooklyn Players lost their theater, they're thinking of performing right here in the Anchorage."

"That's a great idea!" Bess said.

Randy nodded. "Anyway, when he heard us warming up, he asked if we'd ever consider doing the music for one of his plays."

"He actually said something that *wasn't* insulting?" George asked. "I think I might die of shock."

"Not me. I'm too happy," Zoe said. She linked her arm through Randy's, grinning at Nancy, Bess, and George. "Randy is safe and sound, the Heights Gardens benefit is a success, and it's all thanks to Nancy Drew."

# NANCY DREW® MYSTERY STORIES By Carolyn Keene

A MINSTREL® BOOK
Published by Pocket Books

**Simon & Schuster, Mail Order Dept. HB5, 200 Old Tappan Rd., Old Tappan, N.J. 07675**
Please send me copies of the books checked. Please add appropriate local sales tax.
☐ Enclosed full amount per copy with this coupon (Send check or money order only)
☐ If order is $10.00 or more, you may charge to one of the following accounts: ☐ Mastercard ☐ Visa
Please be sure to include proper postage and handling: 0.95 for first copy; 0.50 for each additional copy ordered.
Name _____
Address _____
City _____ State/Zip _____
Credit Card # _____ Exp.Date _____
Signature _____
Books listed are also available at your bookstore.  Prices are subject to change without notice.

760-28